To Lt. Col. Theodore Bothea (?)
Thank you for your tremendous
service and sacrifice to our
country.
Semper Fi
Stan M 4-9--

M000074519

Hill 406

By Stan R. Mitchell

This book is a work of fiction. Names,
characters, places, and incidents either are
the product of the author's imagination
or are used fictitiously. Any resemblance
to actual events, locales, organizations, or
persons living or dead, is entirely coincidental
and beyond the intent of the author.

Copyright © 2019

Fourth Edition

Author's note

This book is dedicated to all of those who have served. Especially those who did their hard time in Afghanistan. To date, nearly 800,000 Americans have served in this country known as the "Graveyard of Empires." Of the 800,000 Americans that have served in Afghanistan since 2001, almost 30,000 have served more than five tours there.

Five tours in harm's way. Five tours of being drawn to the danger and answering the call, multiple times.

What kind of person does five tours in Afghanistan? What causes such a mindset? What creates that kind of service before self?

Hill 406 explores this topic. A few things about this book...

I've obviously written a work of fiction about the Marine Corps and the war in Afghanistan. It's (hopefully) both enjoyable and fast moving, and also real and harsh. A fast roller coaster on the one hand, a searing, scalding potato on the other.

Hill 406 should be a lot of fun; a fast read. But it also contains more depth than a lot of those light military fiction books, where the good guys kick ass and go home unscathed. The characters who survive Hill 406 carry more than their gear with them when they return to the States.

With that being said, a few quick details about

the book.

Camp Leatherneck is real.

The stats on deaths and the state of danger in Helmand Province are (sadly) real. The terrain in that province is real. The tactics and weapons are real.

On the other hand, the towns of "Alim Nuaz" and "Gorahumbira" are completely made up. Also, there is no Hill 406. All characters are fictional. And all Marine Corps units named are a creation imagination.

And with all of this out of the way, I sincerely hope you enjoy the story. But please, put your body armor on now. You're going to need it.

Semper Fidelis,
Stan R. Mitchell
SGT, USMC
A/1/8, 1995-99
Proud infantryman

Other works by Stan R. Mitchell

Nick Woods series

- *Sold Out (Book 1).*
- *Mexican Heat (Book 2).*
- *Afghan Storm (Book 3).*
- *Nigerian Terror (Book 4).*

Detective Danny Acuff series

- *Take Down (Book 1).*
- *Gravel Road (Book 2).*

Other works

- *Hill 406.*
- *Hell in the Mountains.*
- *Little Man, and the Dixon County War.*
- *Soldier On.*

CHAPTER 1

Grant Morgan had no idea when he first met Sam Dean that an epic story had begun. Unbeknownst to him, his life would massively change. And so would many others.

Lives would be lost. (A lot of them.) Lives would be saved. (Not nearly enough.) Careers would end. Careers would begin. A court-martial would top it off, though the court-martial could never eclipse the deaths in its importance.

It was a lot to get your arms around, even in hindsight. But that's sometimes how fate works. And sometimes, when two completely opposite men collide, they set up something absolutely beautiful. At least, that's how it went in this case.

Morgan first met Dean inside a dusty, parched machine-gun bunker in Afghanistan. Morgan was barely more than three months into his third deployment to the country.

Morgan was a sergeant — having put in five tough years in the Corps — and he'd been blooded and forged in his previous three combat deployments. The two men met at Camp Dwyer, deep in the Gamir District of Helmand Province.

Helmand Province was easily the most dangerous province in the country of Afghanistan, and it had already taken some of Sergeant Morgan's good friends.

Morgan had seen a lot of shit in his nearly six years in the Marines, and word had it that this new corporal assigned to the platoon, named Dean, had seen a lot as well.

Morgan hoped it was true. He needed an experienced man like a dog needs a bowl of cool water on a scorching day. And fuck was it hot in Afghanistan? Both in temperature and in spilled blood. Morgan couldn't do anything about the heat, but his platoon had already taken too many casualties and needed an additional, experienced leader, like yesterday.

Corporal Dean, Morgan's new man, was sitting behind multiple layers of sandbags and a big .50 caliber machine gun when the two first met. Morgan remembered it well, even though at the time, he had no idea how consequential it would all prove. Dean wore no body armor and had his helmet kicked off by his side. It had been 120 degrees earlier in the day, and it hadn't cooled down much since then, but the rules said you had to wear full body armor while on post, no matter how hot it was.

"You get caught without your gear on while on post, they'll write you up," Morgan said. "Might take a stripe from you."

Dean was sprawled back, his hands behind his head, leaning against a couple of sandbags. The man looked as if he didn't have a care in the world.

"I have had stripes taken from me before," Dean said with a shrug. "Makes no difference to me."

"You catch a bullet with no armor or helmet on, you might think differently," Morgan said.

Morgan was a sergeant, and it was his job to keep the men in line. But Dean, a corporal with five years of service himself, wasn't having it.

"I have been in enough tight spots to know that when it's your time to go, it's your time to go. I think I'll just keep my flak jacket off. It's hot as hell out here."

Morgan wasn't sure what to say. He was in charge, and he knew he could order the man to put on his armor, but he also knew that Dean was a corporal and probably didn't deserve to be ordered around as if he were some lowly private first class, brand new out of boot camp. Plus, it wasn't really how he wanted to start things off with a fellow leader.

Dean made his move before Morgan could decide what to do. Dean turned around and studied Morgan.

"I see you're wearing all of your gear," Dean said. "You're buckled up tighter than a tanker in the reserves, out on his first combat patrol."

Morgan was indeed buckled into his body

armor and helmet, even though it was still hot enough in the dusky darkness to cause him to sweat like he was in a sauna. Must have been at least ninety, even with no sun, and Morgan's shirt was soaked through. He sort of agreed with Dean that wearing armor was probably overkill, especially behind the sandbags in the fortified bunker. Hell, it hadn't cooled off much.

A light wind at least graced the air now, but it felt like a warm hairdryer blowing lightly across your face. It could've been worse: they had suffered several damn sandstorms that had popped up with no warning. The sand from those blistered and peppered any exposed skin, and they truly made the Helmand Valley feel like hell on earth.

Morgan hated to admit it, but the truth was that the chances of attack at Camp Dwyer weren't too high — the ground around the base was flatter than Kansas, with no trees or cover to be found — but Morgan didn't want to completely capitulate to Dean's words. Morgan finally muttered, lamely, "I follow the rules."

"Suit yourself," Dean said, and then he promptly turned away, ignored Morgan, and re-crossed his hands behind his head, watching his sector.

Well, that was a hell of an introduction, Morgan thought. He had no idea what to do. Whether to be an ass, and order Dean to put his armor on? Or to let it go. At least this one time.

He decided on a different tack.

"How come you not report in?" Morgan asked. "That's what new guys do when they arrive at a new unit. You ought to know that, and you ought to know that I'm the platoon sergeant until Staff Sergeant Hester gets back from that re-supply run, which is going to be a long while."

Dean turned again.

"You're just a squad leader, same as me. Quit trying to pull a power trip. You're nothing more than an acting platoon sergeant. I met the men. I grabbed a shift on the line. Wouldn't have a hard time explaining that to anyone who listened to your shit."

Morgan considered grabbing Dean by his neck and knocking his teeth down his throat. But Dean was tall and lanky. He had strong-looking arms, showing beneath his t-shirt. The man looked as if he could handle himself.

Morgan, on the other hand, was stocky. He was thick, built like a bulldog, but average in height. A confrontation in the tight machine gun bunker would be a hell of a scrap, but truthfully, it was too hot to be scrapping in this hell hole.

Besides, Dean was right. Morgan was only acting platoon sergeant. And though he knew nothing about Dean's reputation, the new transfer was clearly a good leader since he had taken a watch for his squad on his first night with the unit. Dean could have easily skated out of duty for at least a night or two.

Nonetheless, Morgan still couldn't completely let go of the comment about him pulling a power trip. Not on Dean's first day with the unit. Besides, Morgan wasn't the kind of guy to pull a power trip with rank.

"Look, I'm not trying to pull a power trip," Morgan said. "I'm just trying to do what's right and follow the rules. Acting platoon sergeant or not, that's how I've gotten to where I am, and that's how I'll get to where I'm going. We follow the rules in 3rd Platoon."

"I thought you got that rank by charging into a compound to rescue two wounded men?" Dean asked. "Earning yourself a bronze star in the process?"

"I just did what any man would've done," Morgan said.

"Whatever you say, chief," Dean said, and the man never looked back at Morgan.

Morgan let the comment go, and he also let Dean keep his armor off while on post. The bottom line was it was too damn hot and they weren't going to get attacked.

Morgan exited the machine gun bunker, shaking his head, utterly perplexed and amazed at the new man in his platoon. And so began what would come to be his unbreakable bond with Dean. Neither man had any idea on that blazing-hot night just how significant their uniting would prove.

Sometimes, things truly do happen for a reason.

CHAPTER 2

One week after Morgan met Dean, their platoon — 3rd Platoon — was assigned a mission to find a high-value target of the Taliban.

The mission screwed up their time off; something they had been waiting on — and looking forward to — for two months. The platoon had been scheduled for another three days of mostly rest at Camp Dwyer. Nothing like showers and a little time off following a brutal couple of months in the field, but orders were orders.

"Fucking Corps," Dean muttered as the men loaded up into helicopter sticks.

Helo's were supposed to arrive in twenty minutes, but given how most things went, both in the Corps and *especially* Afghanistan, that twenty-minute wait could stretch to six hours. And if it did, not a single man in 3rd Platoon would be surprised. No, not even close.

Morgan had grown to like Dean since their first, rough introduction, despite the fact that they were almost nothing alike. In fact, they

11

couldn't have been more different. Morgan was wired tighter than stressed barbed wire, stretched to its breaking point, while Dean was as loose and uncaring as a tangled pile of kite string.

But they shared one big thing in common. Both had hated the Corps as young men and left it to become civilians, who were once again gladly in charge of their own lives. And both had found themselves drawn, and eventually sucked, back into the Corps.

Dean had lasted less than six months as a civilian. He had made it to college — the University of Kentucky — a big dream of his while he was getting shot at in Afghanistan during the first enlistment.

"College girls love to party and I won't be able to beat them off me," he'd once claimed, while a lance corporal, with dreams of becoming a civilian. "They'll love a badass like me over some limp-dick, frat boy."

But things hadn't turned out that way. Not at the University of Kentucky. Nor at any other college, he'd heard from others with similar beliefs prior to their exit.

Dean hadn't fit in at the University of Kentucky. Even though he'd been just four years older than his fellow students, his tattoos, cold eyes, and real-world experience had kept the girls at a safe distance. It turned out girls actually *did* prefer soft, care-free frat boys, who got fat allowances from their rich parents.

Dean hadn't lasted long in college.

He'd been told he had anger issues, and his actions had given plenty of evidence for such an allegation. He'd been thrown out of several classes for outbursts against the professor or other students. And his college career came to a crashing end when he punched a student and knocked three teeth from the boy's mouth.

"He was burning the flag," Dean had said to Morgan.

"It's free speech, they say," Morgan said sarcastically, with anger in his voice.

"The hell it is," Dean said. "Those fuckers don't realize that their speech isn't free at all. They haven't seen how many men we've lost over here for their so-called free speech."

"It's free to them," Morgan said. "They don't have a fucking clue."

"Yeah," Dean admitted. "Yeah, it's true."

Morgan's time as a civilian had lasted longer than Dean's, but he'd ultimately come to the same conclusion about leaving civilian life and heading back to the Corps. Morgan had finished earning his degree at the University of Tennessee, a few hundred miles south of where Dean had gone. And while Morgan had shared many of the same staunch and hard-line political opinions as Dean, Morgan had proven better at keeping his mouth shut and his thoughts to himself.

A Marine who's wired tighter than barbed wire has that ability, after all.

Morgan had done more than simply finish earning a degree in political science. He'd even managed to meet a fine woman, marry, nab a high-paying job in sales, and keep it all together for nearly an entire year, following graduation and tying the knot with his girl Annie. But the job sucked. His PTSD and paranoia were off the charts. And the lack of a sense of mission or meaning for life, in addition to the crushing emptiness he felt from no longer being a part of the brotherhood of the Corps, had eventually led Annie to leave him. She divorced him two months after leaving.

"She leave you for an attorney or something?" Dean had asked a few days ago, when they were talking about their pasts.

"Nah," Morgan said. "She didn't leave me for anyone. And, I don't even blame her for the decision she made. She couldn't ever get through my walls. And back then, I was drinking every night."

"Missed it that much?" Dean asked, running his fingers through some dry dirt. The two men had gone on a short walk together, and now knelt, talking.

"Hard to believe, ain't it?"

"You thought of all the men getting their balls blown off over here, didn't you?" Dean asked.

"Every night," Morgan said, reaching for a clod of dirt. "The hell of it was I missed it the most when things were going well. When things were at their best. I'd be taking a hot shower or sleeping in that soft bed next to Annie — and damn she had a killer body like you wouldn't believe — but I'd just start feeling guiltier than hell."

"Survivor's guilt," Dean said.

"Yep," Morgan said. "Like, why did I survive to get all that, and not so many others? And why had I not re-enlisted? Was I chicken shit?"

"Nope," Dean said. "But you never feel like you did enough. Or were brave enough. You get out because it sucks balls being in, but then you miss this fucking shit. You feel like a sellout. A quitter."

"I just couldn't stay home any longer when there was still fighting that needed to be done over here," Morgan said. "I watched the news about every night, keeping up with the battles and casualties over here."

"Yep," Dean said. "I had a Google alert for news about Afghanistan."

Dean spat a stream of Kodiak to the ground. The tall, lean corporal was addicted to the wintergreen taste of the dip, and the hit it provided.

Dean wiped his lower lip and said, "They don't fucking get it."

"Who? The women?" Morgan asked.

"No. Any of them. None of the civilians get it."

"No," Morgan agreed. "No, they don't."

They had talked about their pasts in the early morning, while the men were cleaning weapons, and while the sun was rising up and already scorching the dry sand of the Helmand Valley, which was really nothing but a desert floor. The two squad leaders had knelt alone, next to each other, keeping their distance from the men, but also keeping their eyes on the men.

After the orders had come down from higher headquarters to find the Taliban high-value target, and after the men had scuttled off to get their gear ready, Dean and Morgan had remained behind.

Dean had asked Morgan, "Think anyone will die on this hair-brained mission?"

"Maybe," Morgan said.

"Serious question," Dean had asked. "You enjoy being here?"

"Fuck no," Morgan said, laughing.

"But you don't enjoy being home either?"

"Yep," Morgan said.

"Ain't that some shit?" Dean said.

"It is," Morgan said. "It is indeed."

Dean scratched the back of his grime-covered neck.

"Maybe the helicopters will be on time today," he said.

"Maybe they'll pin captain's bars on your insubordinate ass today," Morgan said.

"Fat chance of that," Dean said with a smirk.

"Exactly," Morgan said.

CHAPTER 3

The helicopters arrived only forty minutes late, which wasn't that bad, all things considered.

Third Platoon was flown a few miles away, to a landing zone approximately a thousand meters from a small clump of buildings near Marjah. Marjah was a town of a hundred thousand people, but it was spread out and sparse in its density. It hardly felt like a city or town, really.

And Marjah had been taken and supposedly pacified by the British and the Marines. They had been replaced by the Afghan Army, who held the city now. But like most places in Afghanistan, the Taliban had never truly been uprooted or driven out.

Some days Marjah felt safe. Other days it didn't.

Third Platoon was to patrol through the small village they had landed a thousand meters from. The small clump of buildings that was their target consisted of fifteen different huts and compounds that the platoon had studied by map and aerial photos. Their mission was the same old same old: they were to clear the buildings and search for any Taliban that might be in the area. Or any weapons that may have been hidden, since it was rare to *ever* catch a Taliban fighter alive with weapons.

The final part of their mission was to talk to locals about the high-value target. Some moron in headquarters wanted 3rd Platoon to ask the local villagers about the high-value target.

Morgan and Dean knew that it'd be a waste of time. No local would talk. This mission, like most deployments, would be a total waste.

Well, it didn't really matter. You went where they told you to go, and you did what they told you to do. That was the way things had been in the Corps for at least a couple of hundred years.

Wasn't like they had a whole lot of men anyway. Third platoon was down to two squads — Morgan's and Dean's. Besides the two squad leaders, Staff Sergeant Hester, the platoon sergeant, had returned from his re-supply run to help lead the men along with Lieutenant Gill.

Hester, like any good platoon sergeant, followed the lead of Gill. Gill, the only officer of the platoon, had come to Afghanistan as a brand-new second lieutenant, intent on winning the war. But with nearly a full squad of men either killed or wounded in less than three months, he had lost most of his starch. Gill was focused on keeping his men alive now.

None of the men knew if this clearing operation would be a total misfire or a full-scale, terror-inducing battle. Most of the time, the Taliban were long gone by the time the Marines arrived anywhere. No one knew if they heard about operations from Afghan Army advisors or if they just had a great early warning system in place from the dozens of radio-carrying men and young boys throughout the province, who tracked the paths of helicopters and convoys.

Lieutenant Gill had split his understrength platoon into two maneuvering squads under the command of Sergeant Morgan and Corporal Dean. Gill then kept a small group of men with him as a command element. This command element included himself, his platoon sergeant Staff Sergeant Hester, a radioman, and the platoon's medic (or corpsman). If any fighting happened, it would be primarily Morgan's and Dean's squads that did the fighting.

Not that any fighting happened on this day. On the question of whether this clearing operation would be a total misfire or a full-scale, terror-inducing battle, it proved to be the former: a total misfire.

The men landed, they searched, they found nothing.

It was a typical day of "combat" in Afghanistan. You worked your ass off, while also sweating it off, and usually, nothing happened. Unless you managed to piss off the local villagers, which you usually did.

Today's mission proved a total bust at finding any Taliban or weapons. The two squads maneuvered, covered each other, and climbed walls half-scared out of their minds. But the fear proved unnecessary.

Not a single thing happened, except a man in Morgan's squad named Hunt nearly shot a goat. The goat had emerged from the shadows of a compound and scared the shit out of Hunt, and Hunt had snapped the safety off his M4 and nearly fired at it.

After 3rd Platoon cleared the cluster of huts and talked with a few of the elders, who said nothing, they pushed through to a small hill and set up a defensive position. It was hot, the men were soaked with sweat, and there wasn't a Taliban member to be found for miles. At least not one carrying a gun. They never were to be found with weapons, unless they held all the cards.

Morgan remembered a salty Sergeant Major being asked once on exactly how the Marines would know if the men they came into contact with were Taliban or not.

The Sergeant Major had chuckled.

"How do you know the Taliban from the local population? Well, for the most part, you don't. Not until they start shooting at you anyway."

And it was true. The situation in Helmand Province was incredibly complicated. More than four hundred British or American soldiers had been killed in this province; more casualties than any other province. Morgan didn't even know what the most recent, up-to-date stats were, but it was quite a bit higher.

Helmand Province was a land of opium and marijuana. It was one of the major sources of cash for the Taliban.

As such, the Taliban had plenty of warriors in the area. But the Taliban also paid some of the locals, who weren't Taliban, to fight the Americans as well.

In addition to the quite-capable Taliban, there were local drug lords, with their own fighters.

The Marines referred to almost all fighters as Taliban. The one trait the Taliban, locals, and drug lords shared was they didn't want to fight the Marines when the Americans were ready to fight. So the bad guys of all stripes employed guerilla attacks instead.

They ambushed on some days. Ran on others. And almost always hid their weapons and pretended to be simple farmers or villagers.

IED's, or Improvised Explosive Devices, created the biggest threat in Helmand Province. Marines spent the biggest part of their time on patrol searching for them.

The bombs were made from explosives or fertilizer, sometimes up to forty pounds of it. And a regular ole' wooden board was usually buried in the ground over the explosive. If a Marine stepped on the board, he closed an electric circuit and caused it to explode.

IEDs were everywhere. The Taliban paid civilians ten dollars per IED to plant each one, and ten dollars was serious money in Afghanistan, especially in poverty-stricken Helmand Province.

To steer clear of IEDs, the Marines avoided roads and paths. Instead, they walked through fields thick with crops of marijuana or opium. Or they trudged through dirty ditches, brimming with feces and raw sewage. Between the heat and the sixty-plus pounds of armor and weapons, patrolling was a special kind of suffering.

It was hell. Hell on earth. And often, it was so fucking miserable that you didn't even care if you died. Sometimes, you even wanted to.

And, today had been no different. Third Platoon was spent and the men hadn't been sitting down for even ten minutes on the hill when Lieutenant Gill called up his squad leaders, Morgan and Dean.

"We're going to be picked up and taken back to Camp Dwyer," Gill said when Morgan and Dean walked up.

"What the fuck?" Dean asked.

"This can't be good," Morgan said.

The platoon usually went out for missions that lasted two weeks or more. To be called back this quickly? After one day? Just a few hours into their mission at that? That couldn't be good at all.

"We're about to get royally screwed," Dean said.

"I don't know," Gill said. "They haven't told me why."

"That sounds about right," Dean said.

"Watch your attitude, corporal," Staff Sergeant Hester said.

Dean said nothing, walking off and disrespecting the platoon sergeant the same as he had disrespected the lieutenant.

"It's the heat," Morgan said, hanging back. "Just let this time slide."

"I'm about done letting things slide with him," Hester said.

"I am, too," Gill said.

"I'll talk with him," Morgan said. "He's a good man. A solid NCO, who watches out for his men. He's just a little too laid back."

"He needs to learn to keep his damn mouth shut," Hester said, "or I'm going to shut it for him."

Morgan nodded.

"I'll talk with him," he said.

And with that, Morgan jogged off to catch up with Dean, his new friend. The two spoke alone, away from the men, and Morgan told Dean to watch his attitude. Hearing it from Morgan didn't make it any better. Dean simply said, "Whatever you say, man. I'm just saying that maybe if some folks would sack up and speak out against the insanity, the idiotic orders, the constant bullshit, maybe some of this would get better."

"You get to a higher rank, and then you can do that," Morgan said.

"Fat chance of that," Dean said. "I just want to be a corporal. And a trigger puller. AND, a man who's not afraid to speak his mind. I don't plan on changing."

"And you'll never get any real change done as a corporal," Morgan said. "So, you just keep up that attitude and see where it gets you."

"Whatever you say, man," Dean said.

Neither man knew what would soon follow upon their return to base.

CHAPTER 4

Third Platoon arrived back at Camp Dwyer (on the exact same helicopters), staged their gear, and stomped over into a briefing area to meet with the company commander. The platoon members were hot, angry, and anxious — all at the same time. They also smelled like shit.

Their company commander, a captain by the name of Robbins, had seen a lot of men die under his command. Both this deployment and a previous one, where he had served as a lieutenant. Robbins's gray hair was cut short, in a tightly cropped flat top.

He was probably not even thirty years old — none of the men knew his age — but he looked well beyond forty. His face was scorched red by the sun, like worn-out leather, and deep crow's feet lined the corners of his eyes.

The weight of command had nearly crushed him and certainly discouraged him. Rumor had it the man would get out after his current enlistment, despite an exemplary career well on its way to much higher rank. He'd told other officers, according to the rumors, that he'd ordered too many men to their deaths on his two tours, sending the men on pointless clearing operations, because that's what the brass above him demanded. And too often, the only thing his men had found were IEDs and stench-filled, shit-filled ditches. It was all a waste of time, and he was done.

Robbins looked more weary than normal today. Charlie Company, his company, had only roughly a hundred men, and it was supposed to be responsible for a ten-mile area of responsibility, but that was an impossible task. Even the lowest-ranking private knew it.

Captain Robbins wasn't wearing any body armor and he only wore his soft cover for headgear, since he was behind the fortifications of Camp Dwyer's walls. Robbins took off his soft cover, raked a sleeve across his sweat-soaked forehead, returned the cover to its rightful place on his head.

"I'm not going to waste your all's time," Robbins said. "It's too damn hot for that, and I don't have the time. Frankly, you all don't either."

He kicked the hard, sunbaked ground with his boot, studying the dirt. After a moment, he raised his eyes.

"Sometimes in life, we get orders we don't like," he said. "This, gentlemen, is one of those days."

"Spit it out," Dean muttered under his breath.

He wasn't one for theatrics. Or cushioning bad news.

Morgan, standing next to Dean, elbowed his newly-acquired friend. Dean had spoken too loudly, and it wasn't conduct befitting a leader. Not that Dean had ever sweated how a leader should act. At least not from what Morgan had seen so far.

"I've learned today," Captain Robbins said, "that our whole battalion is being moved. We're moving about a hundred miles south, linking up with a British unit, and pushing still further south."

Morgan wondered why if this was the case, the Captain was only briefing 3rd Platoon alone. Why not the entire group of Charlie Company. He knew now — more than ever — that something bad was about to go down to his men.

"Unfortunately, you men won't be going with us as 3rd Platoon," Robbins said. "Our company has taken some heavy casualties, as you all know, and we're going to disband 3rd Platoon and break you all up."

"Fuck me," someone muttered.

"Fuck us," someone answered.

"Shut the hell up," Staff Sergeant Hester said. "Show some damn respect to the captain."

Captain Robbins ignored the dissent. It was probably for the best, Morgan thought.

Robbins continued, saying, "We have two leadership positions that need to be filled in the company. Thus, Lieutenant Gill and Staff Sergeant Hester will be assigned to two different platoons to fill out some missing positions."

Third Platoon was too stunned to say anything more.

Captain Robbins continued, "Lieutenant Gill, you'll be assigned to a new platoon. Charlie Company lost a lieutenant two weeks ago. And Staff Sergeant Hester, you'll be assigned to a platoon in Alpha Company. They've got a new lieutenant, as well, and they need an experienced platoon sergeant there."

Hester nodded. Everyone else was too shocked to react.

The men had trained for months and prepared to wage war against an enemy seeking to destroy them. But to be destroyed by command? In a way that none of them had ever dreamed? Or had any way to even defend against?

It was madness.

"The rest of you men, you'll be split up. About half of you will go under the leadership of Sergeant Morgan and Corporal Dean. You'll create a single squad and be assigned to a logistics unit. There's a heavy truck company that keeps getting shot up. They have plenty of officers and staff NCOs, but they're desperate for more force protection of their convoys from professional shooters such as you men. As such, our battalion commander has been ordered to provide a squad of riflemen. And that shit has rolled downhill and landed on you guys. I wish I had better news, but it is what it is. Those who don't go with Morgan and Dean will be sent off as replacements to fill slots in other shot-up platoons."

Captain Robbins shrugged, apologized, and muttered, "You men are dismissed. Sergeant Morgan and Corporal Dean, you two head to company headquarters so they can work out the details of your link up with the new unit. Last thing we want is some dead Marines while you all travel out to your new base. Your new home."

The words seemed so final. So permanent.

"I'll see you men back in the States," Robbins said. "Make me proud."

And with that, the meeting was over, but the shock was so much that the men were stunned and locked where they stood. No one said anything. No one moved.

"We're being moved to a fucking pogue unit?" one of the men asked. "Or sent off as replacements? Those are our options?"

"This has got to be a joke," another said.

"Logistics? We're in logistics now?" Hunt, one of Morgan's men, asked.

Morgen needed to act before this got out of hand.

"You all heard the captain," he said. "And we're going to do what we're told."

The men failed to respond, so even Dean spoke.

"Stop acting like a bunch of weak-ass bitches,"

he said. "We'll bear up to whatever we're told to do. It's what Marines do. It's what we've been doing since Iwo Jima and Vietnam. We're going to lean into this and get it done, whatever it is."

"We're going to be doing a bunch of working parties, loading boxes and shit," Wandell said. "That ain't fighting. That ain't what I signed up for."

"Shut your mouth," Morgan said, stepping toward Wandell. "I've heard enough bitching. You want to say some more?"

Wandell looked away.

"Anyone else?" Morgan asked.

No one said a thing, but no one appeared pleased either.

"Everyone take five and we'll reconvene," Morgan said.

The men drifted off, but they moved slowly. And no one said a word.

Dean stepped up by Morgan and removed his cover. Morgan noticed Dean's hair was too long (as usual) and needed to be cut, as Dean wiped a sleeve through his too-long locks of hair. Before Morgan could say a thing about Dean's hair, Dean said, "You know the saying, 'As long as the men are bitching, everything is fine. It's when the men stop bitching that you have to worry.'"

"Yep," Morgan said. "I think they could have survived a massive IED better, even if it'd have taken out half the platoon."

"No one could see something like this coming," Dean said. "A fucking truck company? You know the Corps. We won't be riflemen. We'll be helping those fuckers change out tires and everything else before this over. No one joined the infantry to come to Afghanistan to change tires."

"It'll be our job as NCOs to make sure we're not over there changing out any tires or toting oil around for them," Morgan said.

"And we'll be doing it without the firepower of Lieutenant Gill or Staff Sergeant Hester on our side," Dean said. "You've got three stripes on your collar. I've got two. That ain't shit. Every Gunny and Staff Sergeant over there will be bossing us around like we're newbies straight out of Parris Island."

"We'll deal with that when it happens," Morgan said.

Neither of the men said anything for a few moments, both in their own thoughts; both worrying about their new assignments and all the what-if's. They had trained for combat. For infantry maneuvers. But trucks? Big convoys in the middle of nowhere. A pogue unit?

A distant rumble sounded, and it grew into a louder and louder roar. Two jets screamed by Camp Dwyer. F-18s, loaded with bombs.

"Go get 'em," Dean muttered.

It was something he often said when jets flew over the platoon. But it struck a thought with Morgan.

"Seeing those jets, I just had an epiphany," Mor-

STAN R. MITCHELL

gan said, watching the fighters move off into the horizon, flying low and carrying their sound with them.

"What if we're about to really be put in the shit?" Morgan asked. "I remember on my second tour hearing about one of those truck convoys getting shot up pretty bad."

"I don't mind it if they're shooting at me," Dean said. "Beats dealing with IEDs."

It was a common motto in Afghanistan. If someone were shooting at you, you could do something about it. IEDs? At best, you could avoid them. But there wasn't much of a way to fight them. Not as you could enemy infantry, who were firing at you.

Almost everyone preferred to fight an enemy instead of endlessly searching for buried mines that were nearly impossible to find.

But Morgan couldn't shake the memory of the story he had heard. A big 12.7 mm, shooting up the column, along with hordes of fighters up in the hills. The Taliban had even been well-supplied with RPGs, which they had rained down on the trucks and troops.

"Let's go talk to the men," Morgan said, and with that, the two men headed off to find their men; or what remained of their two squads. Neither had any idea how accurate Morgan's premonition would prove.

CHAPTER 5

Sergeant Morgan and Corporal Dean brought their six men to the relatively-plush Camp Leatherneck the very next day. It certainly beat Camp Dwyer, in terms of amenities. And the logistics unit they were going to apparently had pull with command because an empty CH-53 helicopter was dispatched to Camp Dwyer to pick up the eight ground pounders.

One-way empty flights were almost unheard of in Afghanistan, where critical logistical resupplies might take days, but Morgan and Dean accepted the chopper as their new reality.

"Guess we're not lowly grunts anymore, constantly getting shit on and forgotten," Morgan said.

"Bullshit," Dean said. "They're just going to treat us like royalty until they ask us to go charging into some ambush or traipsing up some mine-laden road."

"Probably," Morgan said.

At Camp Leatherneck, a staff sergeant met the

new men and directed them to their quarters. It was a simple general-purpose tent with cots, but for Marines used to sleeping in the dirt, it was solid living.

"Bet the chow will be better, too," said Hunt, as the men threw down heavy packs and sea bags.

Hunt had been assigned for the move along with Morgan and Dean, as well as five others: Anderson, Biggs, Hernandez, Jordan, and Webb.

The men stowed their gear, explored their new quarters (including finding the head, or bathroom, always the most important part), and talked about some worthy finds along the way.

Biggs said he had seen — no shit — four different female Marines. Female Marines were supposed to be treated exactly as male Marines, but the Corps still had a ways to go on that.

"One looked hot as hell," Jordan said. "She had some big-ass titties."

Morgan nearly said something, but then didn't. They were in private, and you can't take warriors off the line and expect them to suddenly be perfectly-spoken garrison Marines. His Marines had barely seen a woman in three months. What could you expect?

The men shot the shit at their end of the tent. Morgan and Dean were staying to themselves on the other side of the large general-purpose tent.

"Guess the men are happy again," Morgan said.

"They went from being sad about leaving the battalion to suddenly stoked about the new sights around here," Dean said. "Guess a pair of titties will do that to any man."

Morgan glared at him.

"I know," Dean said, raising his hands in surrender. "I'll be a good little leader."

"I seriously doubt that," Morgan said. "Just remember that I won't be able to protect your ass over here."

A corporal dropped into the berthing area and said the unit commander wanted to see Morgan and Dean. They walked downstairs, met an old-looking lieutenant colonel, and got the shortest low-down either had ever received in their lives.

Once inside the man's office, the lieutenant colonel said, "I wanted to welcome you all to our unit. We really need you, and we plan to use you. You probably won't even see me again after today, but I wanted to say just a few words. You'll be working for a Captain by the name of Tomlin. I won't sugar coat it. The man's a pencil-pushing prick, and he'll probably never leave the base. A bit yellow, honestly. On the one hand, I probably shouldn't tell you all this. On the other hand, you'll figure all this out in no time anyway. And I'll be honest, you're heading into the shit. We've lost twenty Marines already, and we've got five more months left."

The lieutenant colonel stood, walked over to a map on the wall.

"Our convoys are leaving Camp Leatherneck and as you can see, we've only got a couple of primary routes we can take. When we go this way, we have to traverse through several towns and villages. And we always hit IEDs. But when we avoid the populace, we've got this high rings of hills and peaks on both flanks. We go down the valley and we take fire from the high ground on both sides. No matter what we do, we take casualties, it seems. Worst part is we're convinced there's at least one informant on base. Maybe more. The Taliban always knows when we're coming. And which way we're going."

The colonel walked away from the map and returned to his seat.

"I mentioned that Captain Tomlin is a joke. And he is. But you've also got First Lieutenant Flatt in the unit. She's kick-ass, and more than makes up for Tomlin. You stick by her and you'll be fine. Any questions?"

Morgan had no idea how to respond to such a frank assessment. A shitty officer? Loads of casualties instead of the typical ooh-rah speech, about how no one messes with Marines?

Dean, as usual, opened his big mouth with hardly a care.

"Tomlin's an asshole. Flatt's amazing. And we're going to be in the shit? Roger that, sir," Dean said.

"That sums it up," the colonel said. "We brought you men here because we needed some real shooters in our unit. Not mechanics who can also fire a rifle. You guys help protect my Marines.

And help Tomlin and Flatt figure out how to deal with the Taliban. Good luck."

Morgan said, "Appreciate you shooting straight with us, sir. It'll help us hit the ground running."

And with that, the lieutenant colonel turned and picked up some paperwork. The meeting was clearly over.

CHAPTER 6

The next two weeks raced by in a blur. Captain Tomlin and First Lieutenant Flatt informed Dean and Morgan that they believed it would be best if the men simply accompanied a few convoys and observed, until they got their legs under them and saw how things worked in a logistics company. Dean and Morgan agreed.

And that's exactly what the eight new infantrymen did. They went out on three different convoys and learned the art of transporting tons of supplies through the middle of a war zone in a place where roads were more rare than a politician with good sense.

It was nothing like they expected. And even after two weeks, it was hard to wrap their arms around.

The convoys were massive. Often with as many as seventy trucks, with more than two hundred Marines involved in the long line of vehicles.

The logistics company hauled everything. Ammo. Water. Fuel. And of course food, but the food was less important than the first three.

A Marine could go without food for a day or two. Ammo? Or water, in the scorching heat? Or fuel for vehicles needed for fighting? You couldn't go without those. Not for long.

The convoys had MRAPs, huge vehicles with V-shaped hulls. The angled bottoms of the newly-designed vehicles protected better against mine blasts compared to the flat bottoms of Humvees or regular five-ton trucks. The angled bottoms of the MRAPs guided the blast around the vehicle, instead of directly absorbing it.

MRAPs came in four-wheeled configurations, and a much larger six-wheeled version. The company had a bunch of both.

There were also Husky Route Clearance Vehicles, which looked like some kind of lunar explorer vehicle. These vehicles were typically equipped with mine rollers and were designed to survive massive IED explosions. They sat higher off the ground, so the blast lost much of its power by the time it struck the Husky. And even then, the Husky Vehicles were designed to break apart in a blast, thanks to shearing pins, which allowed for quick repairs on site out in the field.

The mine rollers helped stop mines, as well, and they were attached to the front of numerous vehicles in the convoy. The mine rollers had eight to ten wheels attached to a long, single axle, and the things weighed almost ten-thousand pounds, which helped simulate the heft of a vehicle.

The mine rollers worked wonderfully against IEDs. But they were so heavy that they made the vehicles difficult to drive and maneuver.

Finally, there were wrecker vehicles, because there were always breakdowns or vehicles that hit mines, which inevitably needed to be towed.

The convoys may have been different than how Dean and his men were used to operating, but their tactics were quite similar to those of the infantry. At night, if the convoy hadn't reached its destination, they'd park the trucks in a giant circle; just like the infantry would form up into a circular perimeter.

Also similar to the slow patrols that Dean and Morgan were used to, the convoys barely moved across the landscape. They averaged a slug-like three to five miles per hour.

"I've seen snails move faster," Dean said at one point on their second patrol.

You would have thought the convoys would average ten or twenty miles per hour, but the terrain and lack of roads simply wouldn't allow it. Nonetheless, the first couple of weeks were important for the men to get used to the way of life in a logistics company. They became acquainted with the techniques and tactics of the unit, and also got a better feel for the skittish Captain Tomlin and truly impressive First Lieutenant Flatt.

This would prove an important thing. Because while they had avoided any ugly combat in their first two weeks in the company, their very next mission would be their first operating as a unit tasked with serving as a quick reaction force within the convoy. Their job would be to rush toward anything that happened to the convoy, and all expected action.

It was "go" time, and the men under Sergeant Morgan and Corporal Dean were ready to get some.

CHAPTER 7

The trucks were scheduled to depart the safety of Camp Leatherneck at 0400. Just minutes before it was time to move out, they waited, many of the men and women impatient to go.

It was a massive formation of vehicles, whose engines roared and belched like big tractors waking up for a long day of work. The MRAPs, trucks, and tractor-trailers of the convoy were parked close together, staged together in ranks. Seen from above, the lines of vehicles looked like one side of a chessboard, a rectangular block of millions of pounds of metal, carrying an almost equal amount of supplies and fuel.

But even the lightly-armored trucks were as dangerous as pawns on a chess board, wielded by some grandmaster. They were protected by heavy machine guns that could reach further than anything the Taliban had, they were manned by gunners better trained than any the Taliban had, and they were protected by aerial assets that could see and destroy the Taliban almost at will.

And so the convoy of thirty-plus vehicles warmed up and prepared, coming to life and uncoiling itself from behind the protection of the huge Hesco walls of the base of Camp Leatherneck. The roar of their heavy diesels echoed across the dry ground, like the sound of a sleeping dragon, exiting its lair and looking for any animal foolish enough to take it on.

"No wonder the freaking Taliban only mess with infantry guys," Webb said. "Who would go after trucks with bullet-proof glass, loaded with more fifty cals and Mark 19s than we even have in an infantry company? We're humping around, sweating our asses off, throwing grenades by hand. Or from M203s. These guys are literally shooting 40 mm grenades out of machine guns."

And it was true, but it was too early for anyone to take up much conversation, so his comment died off in the pre-dawn darkness.

Webb was riding in a four-wheeled MRAP with Sergeant Morgan, Hunt, and Jordan. The new infantry guys assigned to the logistics company were assigned two vehicles. Each vehicle had its own driver, assistant driver, and gunner up top. The infantry guys rode in the back of each MRAP, on what were the most comfortable fold-down seats any of the men had sat in since being assigned to the grunts.

The first truck had Morgan, Webb, Hunt, and Jordan. The second truck had Corporal Dean, Anderson, Biggs, and Hernandez. The trucks were in the middle of the convoy, since there was a well-trained route clearance platoon in the lead. They were the experts (relatively) at finding mines and IEDs, as well as solid, firm thoroughfares through which the big trucks wouldn't get stuck in soft sand.

The infantry squad was to serve as a quick reaction force to rush toward any attacks that happened on the convoy. That was a mission that suited Morgan and Dean. Certainly better than what they could have been doing. The cowardly Captain Tomlin had tried to assign each of the infantrymen as simply individual gunners.

"These men are supposed to be expert riflemen and machine gunners," he had said. "They can probably fire those weapons better than our own Marines. We split them up, put them on guns, and it'll allow our own Marines to get off the gun and to serve as drivers and assistant drivers."

"We're not here as replacements," Sergeant Morgan said. "We're here to help you defend the convoys, and we can do that best as a single unit. Or two fireteams working together as maneuvering elements."

"I think he's right," First Lieutenant Flatt said. "If we want to reduce attacks on us, put them in two vehicles in the middle of the convoy. And when the Taliban engages us next time from high ground, let's release the hounds of war and allow these men to go straight at the Taliban. Let's stop just running every time we're ambushed."

Tomlin wasn't having it.

"I want them on machine guns," Tomlin said. "I've spoken on the matter and it's decided."

"You put them on machine guns," Flatt replied, "and their old company commander will have them back in less than a week. Their battalion didn't want to give them up. They were sent to be a part of an innovative strategy to reduce attacks on our convoys. If you'd like, we can ask our own battalion commander for his thoughts on the idea?"

Tomlin could see he was being flanked. And he felt the battalion commander regularly ruled against him, just to be an ass. "The man can't see the prudence of my by-the-book ways," Tomlin thought. "Yeah, I might be cautious, as he's said, but I keep my Marines alive."

But instead of saying what he was thinking, Tomlin said, "Very well. We'll go with your ideas. But you bear the responsibility if any of these men die."

"You don't win a war by turning and running every time you get shot at," Morgan said.

Tomlin ignored him, turning and walking off without another word.

That had been the day prior, and now the squad was in two MRAPs, in the middle of a convoy, waiting to respond to any ambush or danger.

Morgan was watching out the window. It was three inches thick and bulletproof, which combined with the metal around him and the V-shaped hull beneath him, made him feel pretty safe. As long as they didn't take a direct RPG hit or a mortar falling on them from above, they should be fairly safe.

"We're officially in enemy territory," Morgan said, as he watched the vehicle exit the perimeter of the camp.

"Hell, yeah," Hunt said. "I hope we finally get some."

Morgan smiled. He liked the young man.

Hunt reminded him of himself when he was younger. Hunt was the only truly motivated member of Morgan's squad. Dean was only half-motivated, really.

But Hunt? He was a motivator. Morgan had once overheard Hunt telling Webb that Hunt wanted to be just like Morgan. To re-enlist and eventually lead a squad of Marines. Or maybe a platoon someday.

But Morgan's other Marines weren't like Hunt. They were like most Marines, and most Marines wanted out. And who could blame them? The Corps was hell. It sucked pretty much from the moment you stepped on those yellow footprints at Parris Island until you finally drove off base four years later.

Once you got away for a couple of years, you learned that all the hell you went through while serving — absurd inspections, stupid games, ignorant leaders, who didn't have a clue — those were all a necessary part of creating the greatest brotherhood and fraternity in the world. And that such a brotherhood produced the greatest fighting force in the world. But you had to re-enter the civilian world to realize what you no longer had. What you had lost.

Morgan adjusted his heavy flak jacket, which was mostly just a plate carrier. He had the ceramic plates in it and it was heavier than a bitch.

Morgan shifted his eyes from Hunt to Jordan and Webb. Both men were simply leaning against the side of the truck, eyes closed, trying to get some sleep.

Jordan was a tall, lanky guy. He hated the Corps with a viciousness. All he wanted — or talked about — was getting out and going to college.

In some ways, Jordan was like Dean. Dean had wanted to get out and go to college, too. Morgan wondered if Jordan would find out he didn't fit in once he got to college as Dean had. Probably, Morgan figured.

Webb was a different story. He didn't necessarily hate or love the Marine Corps. He was just a walking disaster, who'd probably never even make corporal. And you had to work to not make corporal in the Marine Corps.

Of course, none of this was ever Webb's fault, the way he saw it. The young man was older than most Marines. Had joined at the age of twenty-five, having left rural Mississippi, and having already accumulated three DUIs before he joined.

But he'd tell you at length about how two of them weren't supposed to be on his record. Some judge has messed that up by not filing some form.

Webb had a kid, too. He was two, but Webb and the mother didn't talk anymore. So Webb only rarely heard about the boy or talked about him.

Webb said that was the mother's fault, too. She was a lying, cheating whore, he said. Not the best way to describe the mother of your child. But Morgan had never told Webb that.

Of course, two minutes later, Webb would be telling you about the 18-year-old girl that he had dated before leaving. While Webb was 25. Both the girl, and Webb, had been in a relationship with *other* people. Webb with the mother of his child, in fact. The so-called lying, cheating whore. It was some fuzzy math for sure.

Morgan wasn't sure why Webb thought it was a good idea to bring up his own infidelity. Or why Webb thought a twenty-five-year-old should even be dating an eighteen-year-old, just out of high school. Especially when you were in a relationship. But the man had.

The two had been working at a small barbecue place in a tiny town of a couple thousand. Webb had probably been earning minimum wage, if Morgan had to guess.

But the two had gotten friendly, and then the eighteen-year-old girl had cheated on her boyfriend with Webb. And Webb had cheated on his girlfriend with this very young lady.

Webb wouldn't even say if the girl was a great lay or not, but he sure held her to blame for messing up his life. Apparently, she would flirt with Webb in front of the owner of the small place.

And the owner would get pissed and be super mean to Webb.

"I figure she was doing something with him, too," Webb said.

And in the end, this eighteen-year-old girl had wrecked Webb's life because she called the cops on him when they ended their relationship, or side affair, or whatever you call a twenty-five-year-old dating an eighteen-year-old while in a relationship. She claimed Webb had punched her. And Webb had been forced to spend twelve days in jail because he couldn't be bonded out. That had been the county's fault, Webb had said. They wouldn't let him get access to his cash. Not that Webb had ever had any cash, from what Morgan had seen.

The man spent his money faster than a drunken sailor.

But the girl had cost Webb his job and a $500 ring from the mall that he had bought her, which "the bitch" kept, he spat. Possibly even worse than the job, the jail time, and the cost of the ring, the girl had basically forced Webb to join the Corps, after a judge said to either join or spend a year in the slammer.

"That bitch ruined my life," Webb had said.

Webb blamed the girl for everything, though

Morgan wasn't sure what the girl had to do with the three prior DUIs and assorted screw-ups that had landed him working at a barbecue shop at the age of 25 for minimum wage. He was clueless like that. A total trainwreck who never did any wrong.

Morgan stared at Webb. What a pathetic excuse. How had such a man made it through boot camp?

Webb's trousers weren't "bloused," or wrapped under boot bands on his left leg. Morgan nearly said something, but Webb had his eyes closed. Besides, they were heading into combat, not an inspection.

Morgan went to look away, but then saw that Webb's M4 was off safe.

"Webb!" Morgan yelled. "You stupid, fucking asshole. Put your weapon on safe before the thing goes off."

Webb's eyes popped open and looked down in horror.

"A round fired off in this thing would have ricocheted around and hit at least one or two of us, you damned fool," Morgan said.

"It was on safe," Webb said. "Must have bounced off when the truck hit a bump."

"The truck hasn't hit any bumps," Morgan said. "We only just left base."

"I had it on safe," Webb insisted.

Morgan stared at the man. How many times had he wanted to beat the hell out of Webb? Or wanted to write him up and have him thrown in the brig? But guys like Webb — the worst of the worst — just seemed to somehow survive; to be impossible to get rid of. And Morgan had to try to keep this idiot alive. As well as keep him from killing any of the Marines around him.

The MRAP roared louder and the convoy moved deeper into the countryside.

"Ten minutes into our first real mission as a squad," Jordan said, laughing, "and Webb has already nearly killed his first man."

Morgan said nothing. He just fumed. Fumed at being in a truck company. Fumed at having idiots like Webb under his command. Fumed at the fact he both loved and hated the Marine Corps.

He shook his head. This was what it was really like. This was what you never heard about in books or movies.

But combat soon, he told himself. They'll start shooting at the convoy soon, and that's what you really live for: taking it to the enemy. It was the only thing that made all the bullshit worth it. It was the only thing that made him feel alive. It was the only thing he was good at.

Semper Fucking Fi, Morgan thought.

CHAPTER 8

The convoy ambled on, bouncing and bucking and rocking and stopping. They'd move a bit. Then stop. Then move a bit farther.

It was maddening. The convoy was crawling at a speed that was so slow that it was almost impossible to comprehend. Morgan wasn't even sure they were making three miles per hour.

He tried to keep an eye out the window, looking for Taliban fighters as the sun rose, but he couldn't see well out of the thick, bullet-proof glass. Anything beyond a hundred meters or so was too distorted to make out.

Morgan finally succumbed to fatigue. The vibrating, loud roar of the MRAP's massive diesel engine put him to sleep, as it had the other Marines in his team. Morgan figured Dean and his fireteam were out cold, too.

A change of some kind woke Morgan up at some later point. Or maybe it was his spidey senses. He jolted awake and saw the MRAP wasn't moving.

All of his men were still asleep. Hunt and Jordan were asleep with their heads back against the walls of the MRAP. Webb, the bastard, was lying on the floor, his armor and helmet off.

Morgan stood, kicked Webb hard as hell in the bottom of his boots.

"Wake the fuck up," Morgan said. "I ought to kick your fucking ass, taking your gear off like that."

Webb scrambled to get up and put on his gear again.

"Sorry, Sergeant," he said. "I didn't realize it would be a problem since we were in this big ole' armored thing."

"Shut up with your excuses," Morgan said.

He turned toward the cab, where two logistics Marines were sitting; the driver and assistant driver.

"What's going on?" Morgan asked.

"Truck near the front of the column hit an IED about five minutes ago," the assistant driver said, sounding bored.

"Why didn't anyone tell us?" Morgan asked. "We're supposed to be the reac force if we get hit. Why the hell didn't you tell us?"

"We're not getting hit," the driver said, sounding equally bored. "A truck way up toward the front, probably a mile to our front hit an IED. It's no big deal. Trucks hit IEDs all the time. The explosion only partly damaged the mine roller. They're looking it over now."

Morgan was furious.

"Move us up to the front," he said.

"No can do," the driver said. "We are to maintain our position unless ordered otherwise."

Morgan grabbed his radio, which would connect him to Captain Tomlin and First Lieutenant Flatt.

"Godfather, Godfather, this is Striker 1," Morgan said, referring to Tomlin's call sign. Tomlin had stolen it from "Generation Kill," the HBO miniseries about a Marine Recon unit. Morgan found it particularly offensive that a pogue officer would steal such a call sign; particularly a man who lacked even an ounce of courage. To steal such a call sign from a Marine who served in Recon? One of the most elite parts of the Marine Corps? Just sickening.

"Go ahead, Striker 1," Tomlin said.

"SITREP, over," Morgan said.

"You don't need a SITREP," Tomlin said. "You are to maintain your position, over."

"Request permission to push up and push out from the convoy," Morgan said. "We can provide cover for the Marines at the front."

"Denied," Tomlin said. "Clear the net."

Morgan was furious. Tomlin had basically told him to shut up in front of every member of the logistics company who was near a radio in a truck. And Morgan knew that was pretty much every member. Each truck had one. Those who hadn't heard it would be told of it.

Asshole, Morgan muttered.

"Open the hatch," he said. "I'm getting out of this bitch."

"Are you sure?" Jordan asked. "Might be IEDs out there. And if Tomlin hears about you exiting the vehicle, he'll probably lose it."

"I didn't come to Afghanistan again to worry about avoiding danger or pencil pushers like Tomlin," Morgan said behind him as he climbed down the rear steps.

"Want us to come?" Jordan asked. "I'd just as soon stay here."

"Do what the hell you want," Morgan said. "Wouldn't want you to put yourself at any serious risk."

"Fine with me," Jordan said, taking off his helmet and leaning back against the walls of the truck. Damn, the man was a mini-Dean in the making.

Morgan was disgusted. With Tomlin. With Jordan. With Webb, who was struggling — with great difficulty — to get his armor back on.

"I'll come with you," Hunt said, stepping toward the exit.

Morgan stepped away from the truck, looking up and down the line of vehicles. About thirty yards separated each truck, and the trucks were in a flat area. Some compounds were about a thousand yards to the right. Morgan looked back and saw a few trucks had their gunners covering the compounds with their machine guns. Good, he thought.

He adjusted his armor and walked to the other side of the convoy, pulling his flak jacket down from his neck to adjust it and make it more comfortable. His M4 hung from its sling, pointed at the ground, and his hand was on the pistol grip. He was ready to use it if necessary.

On the other side, he was surprised to see Dean out of his MRAP as well. Dean was leaning against his MRAP, his foot up against the wheel and his helmet off. The man was smoking and his long, out-of-regulation hair blew in the warm air.

Morgan started toward him, hearing Hunt walking behind him.

Dean looked like some kind of dang movie poster. Or some kind of model out in the desert, and Morgan hated to admit it, but he was envious of how cool Dean looked. Tall, good looking, smoking as if he wasn't sweating a damn thing. And in truth, the man truly didn't sweat a damn thing. Morgan was a little envious of that part of Dean's personality, too.

"Nice day, Beautiful," Dean said as Morgan drew near.

Morgan turned to see Hunt was standing near them. He didn't want Hunt to hear what he had to say.

"Hunt, if you're going to be out here, go take a position over there about thirty yards away," Morgan said.

"Yes, sir," Hunt said, jogging off and taking a

prone position.

"You going to chew me out?" Dean asked once Hunt was out of range.

"I ought to," Morgan said. "No helmet? Are you nuts?"

"The British used to not wear their helmets around here," Dean said. "They believed it made them seem friendlier to the local population."

"We're not the British," Morgan said. "What the hell do I have to do to get you to follow the rules and help me set the example. You think I enjoy wearing all this shit? You're going to end up making me write you up."

"I've already got quite a file," Dean said. "And I'm not angling for sergeant, so just do what you've got to do. It'll be no hard feelings. I promise you."

"Damn it," Morgan said. "Just fucking work with me."

"Oh, I will once the shit hits the fan," Dean said. "You'll never see a tougher, meaner, braver bastard than me once the shit hits the fan. But I'm not all about the fuck-fuck games. Or wearing armor when it's completely unnecessary."

Morgan cursed.

"Sorry, sarge," Dean said with a shit-eating grin, throwing in some Army mockery. The Army found no problem with the word "sarge," using it all the time. But the Marine Corps absolutely, under no circumstances, ever used it. It was considered an insult, at the very least.

Morgan shook his head.

"You're going to be the freakin' death of me," he said.

Their radios crackled, preventing Dean from responding.

"All units, this is Godfather. Convoy moving again," Captain Tomlin said.

"Saved by the captain," Dean said.

"It'll probably be the only time he saves your ass," Morgan replied.

"Probably," Dean said.

The two separated and walked toward their vehicles.

"Don't go jumping on any mines," Dean yelled.

"Fuck you," Morgan said, but he said it with a smile. Dean always made him smile. It was about the only thing over here that did, and Morgan told himself that he needed Dean more than he wanted to admit.

Dean helped balance Morgan out, and Morgan needed it. Even Morgan himself knew that he was wired too tight. About everything. Both little and big things.

"Let's go," Morgan yelled to Hunt, who was still in the prone position.

The two men returned to their MRAP, and Dean to his.

The convoy began moving again, but at the same slow, sleepy pace.

"I had no idea riding in convoys would be like riding a really-fast roller coaster," Jordan said.

"Yeah, they're lots of fun," Webb said. "Lots of

fun."

"We could be out humping our asses off," Morgan said, "carrying heavy packs and walking knee-deep in sewage."

The men nodded, and Morgan was grateful neither had responded. He didn't feel like fighting —at least among his own men—today.

The convoy ambled on like a slow-moving band of travelers 170 years earlier, heading west across the plains in crammed, overweight wagons, pulled by exhausted, under-sized cattle. It was slow-going. Torturous and mind-numbing. And there was always the chance of Indians, even on the slowest day.

In less than ten minutes, Morgan could already feel it putting him to sleep. He looked at his men and noticed the same effect. The harsh, noisy diesel engine, and the slow, predictable rocking of the MRAP had a way of putting you to sleep.

Morgan was beginning to fall asleep when his radio crackled.

"Stop the convoy. Stop the convoy. Lead vehicle has hit another IED."

Morgan came awake instantly, and he again asked for his squad to push up, and Captain Tomlin again ordered his men to remain in place.

"What the hell is the point of having us, if he's not going to use us?" Morgan asked, mostly to himself.

Hunt shrugged. Jordan had his eyes closed, not a care but the world, and Webb was trying to fix a strap on his gear. Ever the fuck up, Morgan thought.

This delay lasted nearly an hour. Morgan again got tired of waiting in the MRAP and exited. He and Dean talked for a bit, ate part of an MRE, and finally loaded back up once the call arrived that the convoy was moving.

Morgan would later learn that this IED strike had been worse. Part of a truck had been hit and the company had been forced to tow it. That took a while to set up. But Morgan was learning that just about everything in a truck company took a while. And he was already wishing he was back in his old infantry company with Captain Robbins. This was a complete waste of time. For him. And for his Marines.

The fucking Corps. And the fucking Afghan war. What a bitch.

But it was still early in the story, and Morgan had no idea of the massive train of fate headed his way. He'd be wishing to be this bored again soon. Damn soon.

CHAPTER 9

Captain Tomlin didn't use Morgan's men at all during their first convoy operating alone, and he only barely used them during the second.

Another IED hit the convoy and this time it seriously injured a Marine. Morgan and Dean used their two fireteams to secure a landing zone for a medevac helicopter. Unfortunately, the Marine died before he even arrived at Bagram Air Base.

The Taliban had struck again, killing a Marine without putting a single of their men in danger.

Other than this event, the second convoy was as quiet and routine as the first one. And Morgan and Dean were as frustrated as ever.

"This is such a poor use of us," Dean said.

Morgan agreed, but didn't want to pour fuel on the flames. Dean might go track down Captain Tomlin and tell him what an idiot the man was. But Morgan wasn't happy in the least either. All that they had done so far was ride around like luggage and deploy out of the MRAPs once to secure a landing zone.

Morgan decided to keep it positive.

"We'll find a way to get Tomlin to use us better," he said.

"Sure," Dean said. "And the Marine Corps will double our pay beginning next week."

"Don't be an ass," Morgan said. "Let's think of how we could best be used, in a perfect world. Then, we'll figure out how to make it happen."

Dean surprised Morgan by agreeing, so they spent a couple of days brainstorming. The entire logistics company — Golf Company — was back at Camp Leatherneck refitting and preparing for another convoy.

With a plan in mind, Morgan and Dean tracked down First Lieutenant Flatt and asked to speak to her alone.

The three of them walked away from all the men and women in the truck company. Another mission was looming, and the Golf Company Marines were frantically working on their trucks. Hoods were open, vehicles were being refueled, and Marines were working like madmen, turning wrenches, checking fluid levels, airing up tires, greasing ball joints, loading pallets on trailers, strapping down gear, and hauling ammo up to the machine gun turrets. Marines climbed over and inside their trucks like ants, so much smaller than their massive, looming machines.

Morgan, Dean, and Flatt walked over by a nearby tent.

"What's up?" she asked.

"This ain't cutting it," Dean said.

Morgan shook his head disgustedly. Dean had agreed to let Morgan do the talking since Dean didn't have an ounce of tact. Clearly, the man couldn't keep his mouth shut, even when he had agreed to it prior.

"What we wanted to talk about," Morgan said, "is that we think we're being underutilized."

"Damn straight," Dean said. "What's the point of having us if we're going to ride around like cargo? Not a single one of us has fired a round or done a damn thing since being transferred. And we're approaching a full month with you guys."

Flatt nodded.

"As you've seen, we mostly take IEDs," she said. "Not a lot of direct fire."

"But this is pointless," Dean said.

Morgan grabbed Dean's shoulder and gripped it with the wrath of a hundred gods. Dean winced and shut up, so Morgan relaxed his grip.

"Dean, if you can't control yourself, then I'm going to talk to her alone," Morgan said.

Dean turned, looking angry. But Morgan knew if they didn't win Flatt over, they stood no chance. He had to win this argument, or they'd never even get the chance to talk to Tomlin.

"What we were thinking is this," Morgan said. "We seem to be repeating the same things over and over. We go out, we hit IEDs, and nothing is ever done about those who place the IEDs."

"Of course," Flatt said. "We have a straight-shit job. We move tons of supplies across an IED-strewn landscape. Then we have to turn around and come right back down the same path. And no matter where we are, we're treated like shit by our so-called brother Marines because we're not infantry or combat arms. But you guys have seen in your short time here, we often see just as much shit — or more — than some grunt units."

"Agreed," Morgan said. "We've already noticed that, believe me. But what we're suggesting is, 'Let's change the formula.'"

"How do we do that?" Flatt asked. "You all know the Taliban pays these villagers to plant IEDs. Ten bucks per IED. And ten dollars is a lot of money in Helmand."

"Correct," Morgan said. He could feel her slipping away.

"So how do you change the formula?" she asked.

"You allow us, the ground pounders, to get more aggressive," Morgan said. "Stop treating us like cargo. I mean, we know the areas where they set IEDs. At least in a general sense. Let us sneak out and set up some ambushes."

"Or let us run some patrols," Dean said, cutting in. "Let us search some homes, see if we can't find some supplies. Some of the bomb materials before they go placing it in holes in the ground."

Flatt laughed.

"And you think Tomlin will go for this?" she asked. "Have you met him?"

"Fuck Tomlin," Dean said.

Flatt glared at him. "Don't say something like that in my presence again," she said.

Dean didn't answer but sulked off.

Morgan wasn't ready to give up.

"We're just asking for a little more flexibility and freedom," Morgan said. "We're hunters. Let us hunt."

"My position hasn't changed," Flatt said. "There's no way Tomlin will go for this."

Semper Fi, Morgan thought, as the two walked away. Dean finally couldn't keep his mouth shut anymore.

"This is fucking bullshit," he yelled.

Flatt ignored the remark, and still, unbeknownst to them, destiny raced toward them.

CHAPTER 10

After Flatt turned down their request to change up tactics, the morale of Morgan and Dean plummeted. Truthfully, they were pretty dejected. And for a week, they continued to act as cargo.

Not much happened. And certainly, not much changed.

A convoy they were on hit another IED. A Marine was seriously wounded in an ambush from up in the hills. And again Tomlin barely used the infantry squad assigned to him. The men trained to help prevent such casualties.

But then things changed, and they changed in a big way. And suddenly, it was like Morgan and Dean were on a screaming roller coaster, simply holding on for dear life. The next few weeks rushed by in a blur, and Morgan and Dean sort of played a part, but really played no part at all. They were like helpless, gifted Major League Baseball All-Stars, who were forced to sit the bench, while their team was destroyed by the opposition.

The first thing that happened should have been a big clue. Three different Afghan police forces in three adjacent towns disappeared overnight. Literally, the men who were paid by the government simply disappeared.

They weren't attacked or killed. They simply ran off, taking their weapons, stores of ammunition, and gear. And it all happened on the same night.

Elected officials in the same towns disappeared, as well. Most ran off, but a few fled to Kabul, the capital of Afghanistan. There, they reported that a large Taliban force was heading into Helmand. More than thirty men, all veterans of many battles.

"These are foreigners. Arabs," they said. "Fierce fighters, with a great leader. The Gray Fox. He's leading them."

The elected officials' fear was real, and the Afghan forces relayed the intelligence to the Americans. And that intel arrived without much delay all the way down to Captain Tomlin's Golf Company.

At first, Tomlin played the courageous leader, telling his Marines they had nothing to fear.

But then a massive IED exploded under a fuel truck. It was clearly command-detonated because the convoys had equipment that blocked radio-controlled IEDs. This IED had been done the old fashioned way, with a simple line of wire buried under the ground.

Morgan had found the wire after the explosion, and after what was left of the two bodies had been placed in body bags and evacuated by helicopter. The convoy had waited for a wrecker to come out and drag what was left of the truck back to Camp Leatherneck.

By this point, Tomlin changed. His shaky courage had seen too much. He broke. After all, his vehicle could have been hit in the three-hundred-plus-pound, humongous explosion. The largest one to date.

Suddenly, he told Lieutenant Flatt that because of the threat from such a large Taliban force now operating in the area, he would stay back at Camp Leatherneck so that in case a quick reac force was needed, he could command it and make sure it responded with all due haste.

The Marines of Golf Company knew it was bullshit. Morgan and Dean knew it was bullshit. And Flatt certainly knew it was bullshit. But she was eager to be in command. She had the future rank of general, flowing through her blood. For her, it was a great opportunity. And she trusted her instincts over Tomlin's anyway.

Even Dean, who pretty much believed women shouldn't even be allowed in the Corps, admitted she was as solid a leader as he had seen.

Tomlin did serve one function. He began daily requesting reinforcements. A battalion of Marines. Some tanks. An infantry company. Anything.

His requests were denied. The Marines were all fighting to the south, hundreds of miles away, and until more solid intel arrived, no forces would be moved. So far, Golf Company had only been hit by a large, command-detonated IED. The mysterious Taliban force didn't truly exist, as far as command was concerned.

No one had any idea how wrong they'd be, or how all of this would soon play out. How could they? That's just how life plays out sometimes.

All these setup moves happened within just a few weeks, with Morgan and Dean feeling helpless. They played basically no role in any of it. And while they sat on their hands in complete frustration, the hands of destiny were setting up the pieces that would soon rock their entire worlds and test them as they had never been tested.

CHAPTER 11

Following the massive, 300-pound IED blast, Morgan and Dean strategized. Then they presented a plan to Lieutenant Flatt, since she basically ran Golf Company now.

Flatt had bigger fish to fry than worry about Morgan and Dean, so she signed off rather quickly after hearing their plan.

"I've got three different battalions demanding resupply, Captain Tomlin is practically frozen in fear and staying in his room," she said. "I don't have time to babysit you all. You best not get in over your heads. I'm giving you a lot of leash. Don't fuck me over."

"Aye aye, ma'am," Morgan said.

An hour later, Morgan and Dean stood in front of the men. Everyone wore standard cammies and soft covers, though they carried their rifles slung across their bodies. Inside the wire, the Marines wore standard cammies. But outside the wire, they put on their flame resistant "FROG" uniforms.

Sitting in front of Morgan and Dean, the men

seemed wary. Like they knew their destiny was about to change in a big way. Morgan's men — Hunt, Jordan, and Webb — looked as if they knew what was coming. They had seen Morgan for hours and hours in the MRAP, chomping at the bit to get after the enemy.

Hunt, ever the motivator, wanted to get after the enemy, too. Jordan looked pissed as always. All he ever thought about were women and college. Whatever speech Morgan was about to give would surely interfere with that.

And Webb was his usual disaster of a self. Part of his pay was being garnished for his kid back home, and on top of that, the eighteen-year-old girl was claiming she was pregnant (Webb said it wasn't his; the timing wasn't right). Webb was looking off into the distance, and Morgan wondered what other thing had happened that Webb hadn't informed him of. At least the man couldn't get another DUI while serving in Afghanistan.

Making up the other part of the squad, Dean's three team members were Anderson, Biggs, and Hernandez.

Anderson was a quiet man. Probably not the smartest man in the world, but he did what he was told. (And not a thing more.)

Biggs had been a mechanic before joining. His recruiter had told him he could work on engines in the Corps and then placed Biggs in the infantry. The cruel irony now was that Golf Company needed a mechanic, but Biggs didn't have the certification to do any of the work, so their staff NCOs wouldn't let him do anything, even though he knew how.

All Biggs ever talked about was the 69 Chevelle he owned. He'd talk about it having a 396 big block in it, bored 30 over with 454 heads. No one knew exactly what the hell all that meant, but they knew it was a big engine in a fast car, and that Biggs loved to be covered in grease, working on the damn thing. It's all the man seemed to care about, and it was a damn shame the Corps hadn't made the mechanic.

Finally, there was Hernandez in Dean's team. It was hard to not feel sorry for Hernandez. The man was a talented baseball player, who could easily be playing in the minors, chasing his dream, but a recruiter in the mall told him that the Marine Corps had a great baseball team that Hernandez could try out for.

And that he could be paid better in the Marines than he could in the minors, and still eventually make it to the majors.

The truth was, there were some recreational teams on base in the States, but infantry guys didn't have time to play for those. And now Hernandez was stuck in Afghanistan, damn near suicidal and sick about his decision. Hernandez had wanted to play professional baseball and had thought the Corps would get him a step closer. How wrong he had been.

But this was the team. This was the squad

of eight, who Morgan commanded. They weren't Navy SEALs or some kind of special ops guys. They were normal Americans, who mostly didn't even want to be there.

But these men would bear the cross of serving their country and maintaining the standards and traditions of the Corps, even if it cost them their lives. They would step up to go after the Gray Fox. The motto of Semper Fidelis, Always Faithful, had been beaten into them, and it was more than just a couple of words.

It was a way of life.

"All right, guys," Morgan said. "I know there's rumors about there being thirty-plus foreigners, plus who knows how many local fighters, out there. Might be a hundred men total. And I know some of you are probably scared by that. I might have felt the same way my first tour. Maybe even my second."

Morgan adjusted the sling on his rifle to a more comfortable point on his shoulder. He looked each man in the eye as he did. He had their attention. Every single man was staring at him intently.

"But if we do nothing, they're going to do one of two things," Morgan said. "They're either going to keep picking at us and we're going to keep hitting their IEDs. Or, they're going to mass their forces and try to really take us on somewhere. And if they do this, let me promise you: it will be terrain of their choosing. It will be timing of their choosing. It'll probably be weather of their choosing, when we can't get any air support out. If we let them pick the time and place, they're going to kill a bunch of Marines. Probably even some of us. Ask Dean, he knows."

Dean nodded.

The men respected the word of Dean in some ways more than they did the word of Morgan. Morgan was the company man. He toed the line. He maintained the standards. Dean was the guy who had done his time, but he kept his hair too long, and he wasn't afraid to tell you when the Corps was pulling the wool over your eyes.

"Whether they keep hitting us with IEDs over the coming months, or whether they mass and attack us, either way, they're going to kill a whole bunch of really good men and women. But at a minimum, they're going to kill some of the people we have come to know in the past few weeks here in Golf Company."

A few of the men looked down, Morgan noticed. His words were having their desired effect, and he could tell they knew the truth of what he was saying.

"I'm not sure what you all think about this, but Dean and I aren't willing to sit around and let them hit us. Week-after-week. Time-after-time. We know what needs to be done, and that is this: the best thing we can do is go after them. Keep them off guard. Keep them running scared. Find the bombs before they put them in the ground. We need to be unpredictable. We need to have them scared to sleep at night. Afraid to stage in large groups. We need to keep them off balance."

Morgan looked at the men one at a time, slowly now. Then he sunk in the knife.

"And that's what we're going to do. Some of you may not like it. None of you may like it, except for Hunt's crazy ass. The rest of you though? You probably won't like it. But that's tough shit because this is what we're going to do. And if Dean and I have to kick your ass every single day of the week to do it, then that's what we're going to do."

The men were silent.

"Any questions?" Morgan asked.

Not a single man said a word.

"Good," Morgan said. "Clean your weapons and pack your gear. We're going out in a couple of hours and we're going to hit these bastards right in the mouth."

No one cheered. No one said ooh-rah. Not even Hunt. Well, shit, Morgan thought. So much for the motivational speech.

CHAPTER 12

Sayed Behzad, also known as the Gray Fox, watched as his men entered the small town of Alim Nuaz. The town elder had met him and his fighters at the outskirts and welcomed them warmly.

The men would be sleeping throughout the town, in various homes. This would keep them dispersed in case of a night raid or bombing by the Americans.

If the Americans had intel on the group, the bombing of a home or two wouldn't kill all of Behzad's men. Similarly, if intel to the Americans led to a night raid, then having the men spread out in Alim Nuaz would allow the Afghan fighters (who weren't in the building that was under assault) to encircle and hit the Americans from behind.

There was one other benefit: keeping the fighters dispersed through the town would also keep the villagers from informing on the Taliban fighters of Behzad's. Any town member wanting to alert the Americans would have to find a way to get away from the fighter assigned to their house. Or, "welcomed" to their house.

Technically, his men were invited to stay as long as they wanted in Alim Nuaz. But Behzad knew better than to stay too long. While these villagers claimed to be loyal followers of Islam and supporters of the Taliban, many of them had taken American money. Or worked on American projects. And most just wanted the war to be over.

But no matter how much they might support the Americans, none of them would inform when such a thing often led to the rough, cold-hearted, American special ops folks responding. Those bastards would show up in the middle of the night and treat everyone in the house roughly. The old men. The young men. Even boys. Women. Daughters. All thrown in flex cuffs. All blindfolded and yelled at.

No mother would risk that happening to her family. And certainly no father, who could be whisked away and taken to Kabul, where he'd be thrown in a small cage or some shoddy prison.

Behzad smiled. Yeah, his men would be safe here in Alim Nuaz.

He reached over and scratched his left arm. It was hurting. The arm had been nearly blown off in an airstrike and it was practically useless.

An American fighter jet — or drone — (Behzad never knew which) had bombed Behzad and his best friend Hafizullah. The two men had been riding motorcycles to town when a shrieking explosion flung them from their seats. Hafizullah had been blown into literally pieces. Clearly, he had been the target.

But the explosion had caught Behzad, too, and it had cost him his arm, though a rough surgeon had stapled and stitched it up. But it mostly hung from his body. It was practically worthless.

Behzad spit on the ground. The fucking Americans. Up till that point, Behzad had actually been nothing but a farmer. A simple man who wanted to do nothing but farm and take care of his family.

His friend Hafizullah had also been a farmer. Behzad would have known if the man was involved in any type of operations. The reality was the Americans had probably bombed them because they were riding motorcycles: one of the preferred modes of transportation for the Taliban.

Motorcycles were inexpensive, could maneuver on the washed-out roads that were practically non-existent, and could be hidden under the cover of trees quite easily. They used little gas and made very little noise. The perfect vehicle for Taliban messengers and spies.

But Hafizullah and Behzad had been riding motorcycles that day to check on a village boy who hadn't come home the night before. Maybe he had stayed in the next village over. Maybe he had fallen and broken his ankle up in the mountains. Maybe he had been killed by an American patrol — there had been quite a few in the area. Or maybe the Taliban had taken him to force him into working for them as either a spy or soldier in training.

That was all Hafizullah and Behzad had been interested in before that explosion ripped their lives apart.

Hafizullah got a mournful funeral and Behzad soon found himself depressed from being unable to work with his worthless arm. A village elder had told Behzad that Allah surely had plans for him, or he would have been killed in the strike as well.

Behzad wasn't overly religious, but he'd soon found himself on a journey of self-introspection. And that journey had led to him traveling across the border to Pakistan. Behzad couldn't afford to do a pilgrimage to Mecca, but he certainly could afford to spend time at a madrassa (or religious school) in Pakistan.

That pilgrimage got extended from one week to three years, as Behzad found himself drawn to Islam in ways he would have never imagined. His beliefs led to him joining the jihad against the Americans, and for years since, he had led many brave Afghan and Pakistani men against the westerners.

These days, his strict religious beliefs had led to more and more foreigners joining him. Behzad was far more strict in his views of Islam than even the Taliban.

But there would be time to teach the faith stronger after the war. For now, Behzad mostly kept his intolerant views to himself. There would be time to institute harsh sharia laws at a later point.

Right now was about victory. And for him, that victory would happen soon.

The Taliban had learned that convoys were regularly leaving the American base known as Camp Leatherneck. They were poorly guarded and the Taliban had been given a limited number of wire-guided missiles from Iran. Never had such weapons been used in Afghanistan.

Soon, Behzad would hit a convoy with a dozen missiles. Those Marines who survived would be overrun by his fighters. And the Taliban would record the entire thing. It would be the greatest victory Islam had secured in years. Maybe decades.

Soon, Behzad said to himself. Soon.

For now, he needed sleep. And to rest his aching arm. He'd pay the Americans back for their bombs. He'd pay them back as they had never been paid back, Allah's will be done.

CHAPTER 13

"You want to do what?" Lieutenant Flatt asked.

"We want to run a patrol through the town," Sergeant Morgan said.

Morgan and Dean had aggressively been running patrols for days. The two fireteams had been going out in their MRAPs, running route recons, but they hadn't had any real results.

No gunfights. No villagers caught in the act of planting IEDs. No real tangible success that the men could see. Just plenty of headaches and "almost's."

The squad had *almost* caught two villagers planting an IED, but it had turned out to only be a broken-down car. They had *almost* gotten into a big firefight with a group of Taliban, but the fighters had run off and escaped into a wadi, which had led to an underground tunnel.

Even Morgan wasn't crazy enough to enter a tunnel without reinforcements. And without having higher notified and ready to send out a quick reaction force. That was something Camp Leatherneck didn't currently have, with all the fighting happening far to the south.

Morgan and Dean's men *were* the quick reaction force, so they hadn't pursued the Taliban fighters into the tunnel.

But the patrols were working better than most of the men could see with their own eyes. Despite the lack of firefights or immediate results, the Taliban chatter on their radios showed that the enemy was wary. And they were getting increasingly frustrated. The Taliban were afraid of the unpredictable patrols. In fact, they had nearly been caught off guard several times.

At least that's what the radio traffic said.

Now, Morgan and Dean were asking Flatt for more leash. The patrols weren't doing enough. And the two men wanted to enter the town of Alim Nuaz. The town was the most dangerous place on the map near Camp Leatherneck.

It was about an hour away, but there were always IEDs nearby. And you could see in the villagers' eyes every time you passed near the town a single theme: you are not welcome.

"There's no way I'm signing off on a patrol into Alim Nuaz," Flatt said. "That'd be like signing your all's death warrants."

"We won't do anything stupid," Morgan said. "We'll just show the flag. If we're lucky, someone will fire on us."

"If you're lucky?" she asked. "That doesn't

sound like luck to me."

"We're infantry," Morgan said. "We don't mind some combat."

He was smiling and Flatt looked as though she wanted to kill him.

"What would be gained by someone firing on you?" she asked.

"If we're fired on," Dean said, jumping in, "we can get aggressive, enter some homes, maybe find some bomb-making materials."

"You know that place is just loaded with bomb materials," Morgan said. "They hit Golf Company every time you guys drive through there."

"Every time *we* drive through there," she said. "You forget you guys are a part of Golf Company now."

"Yes, ma'am," Morgan said. "My mistake."

Flatt sighed.

"So, you show the flag, maybe get shot at, raid a couple of homes, and maybe grab some bomb materials? Seems really risky without much hope of payoff."

"We keep them off-balance," Morgan said. "Now they're thinking about having to defend Alim Nuaz against the next patrol, instead of planning their next attacks on us. Just a simple switch from defensive to offensive warfare."

"You'll only have eight men," she said.

Morgan could tell they were winning the argument, so he poured it on.

"We'll have eight men and two MRAPs. And they'll have fifties on them. Nobody in their right mind is going to mess with us."

She wasn't convinced, so Dean piled on.

"There's never been an American force completely overrun except for some of the bases out on the border," Dean said. "And the Taliban had planned those attacks for months. This is completely different. They have no idea we're coming. We'll be fine. There's no way they'll overwhelm us, though it'd be nice if they tried. We'd probably kill a bunch of those bastards then. Believe us, we'd rather duke it out in a firefight than keep running over bombs buried in the ground."

"I'm not completely convinced, but I'm also not an infantry commander," she said. "Plus, I have way too much to do to argue with you. This is your all's area of expertise. If you all want to go, go. Get me your plan, with a contingency option written up in it in case something goes wrong, and I'll sign off on it."

"Yes, ma'am," Morgan said. "We can't ask for more than that."

CHAPTER 14

Two MRAPs sat on the outskirts of Alim Nuaz, parked alongside each other, their menacing .50s aimed toward the buildings in front of them. The drivers of the MRAPs kept plenty of distance between them — about thirty yards — just in case there were any IEDs. And while they weren't expecting any IEDs, better safe than sorry.

It was an hour's distance to Camp Leatherneck, and if one MRAP exploded, they wanted to at least have another vehicle they could escape with. Flatt had ordered Morgan to have an evasion plan in place in case one MRAP took a fatal hit. Morgan came up with one, and the plan was simple: the infantrymen would grab the fifty, all ammo and other removable stuff, and exit the area. A convoy would then head out from Leatherneck to rescue the stranded MRAP, which would be pulled or placed on a trailer back to base.

Frankly, though, Morgan wasn't the running kind, so there'd be no evasion or abandoning of any MRAPs.

"No movement ahead now," a machine gunner said from the turret in the MRAP Dean was riding in.

The machine gunner was a man by the name of Rayho. The guy seemed solid to Morgan, and Rayho had a good reputation.

"You don't see anything?" Morgan asked. "Not them boys, either?"

"Nothing now," Rayho said.

A few young boys had gone running into the town as the MRAPs pulled up on the edge of Alim Nuaz. Morgan knew they had lost the element of surprise, but the Taliban had probably not had time to place any IEDs. That's what he was counting on, anyway.

"Drop the ramp," Morgan said. He pushed a button on his radio. "Bravo team deploy."

Both teams pushed out from the back of the MRAPs and took up positions in a wide line, facing the town. Some men took a knee, others went into the prone. And while they scanned the walls ahead with their RCOs, or Rifle Combat Optics (scopes with 4x magnification), Morgan studied it with a pair of big binoculars. He had 8x magnification, and he studied the walls and openings in the buildings with great care.

"See anything?" Dean asked, walking up behind him.

Morgan didn't lower the binoculars but continued studying the ground ahead while he answered.

"Nothing yet," he said, "but they're in there."

The Taliban, and especially the villagers, were bold in Alim Nuaz. White flags — the flag of the Taliban — flew from most of the homes.

"Fucking bastards with their flags," Dean said. "Love to come in here with a company of Marines."

"You'd never get through it," Morgan said. "They'd see you coming, or know you were staged nearby, and the place would be covered with IEDs."

"You're probably right," Dean said. He spat on the ground and twisted around, stretching out his back.

"We get one shot at this," Morgan said. "And then never again. They'll be waiting for us next time."

"Then let's make the best of it," Dean said. "Let's not sit on our asses long and allow them to set up. Let's get in there."

Morgan dropped the binoculars and glared at Dean.

Dean laughed and walked back to his fireteam.

"Load up," Morgan yelled. "We're going in."

CHAPTER 15

Sayed Behzad, the Gray Fox, had a pair of binoculars, too, and he watched the two MRAPs as men piled into them.

"Who are they?" he asked the man next to him.

"The boys say they're Marines. Not soldiers. Marines from out at Camp Leatherneck."

"The group that's been harassing us? Running patrols?" Behzad asked.

"Yes," the man said.

"Why have our informants on the base not kept us apprised of these men and their patrols?"

"Our spies say they aren't really a part of the truck company. These men pretty much do as they wish."

Behzad grunted. There were only two MRAPs out there. Eight men were all he had seen. Were they really coming into Alim Nuaz? Surely not.

The big machines belched smoke and rolled toward the main road into town.

"We can take these men out," Behzad's companion said. "This is our chance to finish them."

Behzad considered the idea.

"Check in with our spotters again," he said. "Surely more troops are rolling or flying toward Alim Nuaz."

The Taliban had plenty of loyal men through Helmand who called in all movements of American troops, from planes soaring overhead to convoys and helicopters. Behzad's comrade screamed into the radio, yelling at the watchers throughout the valley for new updates. Again and again, men replied in the negative. No other Americans were coming.

"We have thirty men," the companion said, after the final check-in from the watchers. "We can take this unit. Plus, we could get the local villagers to help. There's probably another twenty or thirty men who would fight."

Behzad shook his head "no."

"We will not," he said. "Our task was to ambush a convoy, not fight with ground troops. Who cares if we kill eight men. That's a minor victory. Tell the men to hide and not to engage under any circumstances."

"And if they find the missiles?" the companion asked.

Their prize possession of wire-guided missiles was in the middle of the town plaza, locked behind a simple door.

"If they find the missiles, we fight to the death to protect them," Behzad said.

His companion smiled, bowed, then ran out to spread Behzad's orders.

CHAPTER 16

Sayed Behzad was wrong about the number of Marines entering the town. There were a driver and assistant driver in each vehicle, plus the two gunners on top.

Additionally, Dean's MRAP carried a medic, though the corpsman had *no* plans to exit the vehicle under any circumstances. Morgan's MRAP had another man, as well. He was an Afghan interpreter, and he also had no plans to exit the vehicle. But his ear was locked on a radio in front of him, and he was listening to all the transmissions going on by the spotters and Taliban in the area.

"This is very bad, man," he said to Morgan. "Many Taliban in the area."

He pointed to the radio.

Morgan shrugged. He hoped there were many Taliban in the area.

"You crazy, mon," he said, pointing to Morgan.

Morgan smiled. "We are," he said. "And you sound Jamaican."

The interpreter looked confused. "What is Jamacant?," he asked, messing up the word, as he messed up so many English words.

"Never mind," Morgan said. "You just tell me if they say anything that matters."

Morgan's MRAP led the way down the main, dirt road of Alim Nuaz. The MRAP moved slowly, less than five miles per hour.

"I don't like this," the driver said.

A few Afghan men stared at the big truck. They were tall, bearded, and defiant looking. They wore green robes with long sleeves, which reached to the feet. Most villagers — and Taliban — wore these in Helmand. They were called "manjams," and the Afghans usually wore white turbans with them.

All of these men wore white turbans.

"This is some scary shit," the driver said. "They are just staring at us."

"Shut up," Morgan said. "Rayho, you hanging in there okay?"

"Roger," Rayho said. "If one of these fuckers makes one false move, I'm letting them have it with this fifty."

The turret moved to cover another group of men.

"Everyone just stay calm," Morgan said. "Don't show them an ounce of fear."

Dean came in over the radio.

"Want us to deploy?" he asked. "If a single RPG is fired from one of these alleys, we're fucked."

The MRAPs they were traveling in didn't have

an RPG net (or bar armor) around them. The netting or bars might have helped the vehicles survive an RPG strike, but these two MRAPs didn't have them.

Morgan was aware of this — he wasn't an idiot — but dismounting his men posed its own risks. It would force the MRAPs to not be able to floor it and escape if an attack happened. Instead, they'd have to wait on the troops to all load and be accounted for.

Additionally, if the men deployed, there was a greater chance of contact. Some Taliban fighter or villager might take a potshot at one of the men, whereas they wouldn't with the MRAPs. Firing an AK at the MRAPs would be like shooting a slingshot at a massive Rhino: a total waste of time and a good way to die.

Dean wasn't happy with the hesitation from Morgan.

"What was the point of entering Alim Nuaz if we're just going to drive through and not do a damn thing?" Dean asked.

They were using squad radios, so no one higher could hear Dean. That was good. But the freedom of squad communications meant Dean didn't hesitate to fire off from the hip. And the squad members each had earpieces and radios, too, so they could hear Dean undermining Morgan.

"Our mission," Morgan said, anger and fire in his voice, "is to show the flag and investigate anything we see that's suspicious. You helped write the order, so stop acting like a total asshole."

Dean didn't answer that. Morgan's lead MRAP worked its way down the primary road. Most of the villagers were inside, and other than the boys at the edge of Alim Nuaz, and the fierce men who had stared down the vehicles, there was no one to be seen.

"This is scary as hell," the driver said. "Place is like a ghost town. We're about to get hit."

Morgan felt the driver was probably right. There should have been more people out, and the town elders *should* have approached them. The town elders usually wanted to get a feel for the Americans; find out why they were there and how long they'd be staying.

The road curved to the left. Tall walls flanked the road, with occasional small openings. As Morgan's MRAP went around the bend, still moving nice and easy, the road opened up on the sides into a wide plaza. It wasn't green or nice — nothing like a park — but it was a wide, sandy dirt plaza. And in it were four white Toyota trucks.

"What the hell do we have here?" Morgan asked the men in his first MRAP.

"We've got four pick-up trucks ahead," Morgan said into the squad radio.

"Those have got to be Taliban," Dean said. "No villager can afford a truck around here."

"My thoughts exactly," Morgan replied, though he nearly said, "No shit, Sherlock." Morgan was still irked by Dean's undermining on the radio from earlier. He'd talk to the man about that when they were alone. Of that, he was certain. But for now, there were more pressing matters.

"Everyone out," Morgan said into the radio. "Let's deploy, and get that second MRAP up here alongside us to cover the square."

The eight Marines exited the MRAPs and spread out in a line. As they pushed toward the trucks, their rifles up and ready, the two MRAPS behind them pulled into overwatch positions, their big fifties covering the trucks.

Morgan carried his M4 in the ready position, pulled tight into his shoulder. He was toward the center of the line, with Dean just off to his right.

He kept his weapon aimed toward the trucks. Were there men in them, hiding in the beds? Or could they be bombs?

"Everyone stop!" he yelled. "Stop where you are, and get the hell down. All the way into the prone."

His men obeyed, except for Dean.

"You, too, Dean," Morgan said. "Might be a bomb in one of them trucks. If I go down, the men will need a leader to get them — and what's left of me — back."

"Let me do it," Dean said, "and you stay back."

"Do what I fucking say," Morgan said, ignoring the man. "For once, just do what I fucking say."

Dean went down to the prone like the rest of the men. They were a good forty yards back, but even at that distance, if there were IEDs in the trucks, it might not be far enough away. But getting low might be just enough.

CHAPTER 17

Sayed Behzad watched the lone American approach the trucks from the room of a high building several hundred yards away. He was standing at a mud, cut-out hole, which served as a window, hiding back in the shadows and using a pair of Russian binoculars more than thirty years old.

"Did anyone leave anything behind in the trucks?" Behzad asked his companion.

"There shouldn't be anything," his companion said.

"You should have checked them," Behzad said. "And you shouldn't have allowed the men to park four trucks that near each other. The trucks should have been spread out and hidden under old tarps."

"Yes, sir," the man said.

Behzad studied the trucks. Was there anything in them? Any clues about the thirty Taliban fighters in Alim Nuaz? Or, more importantly, about the missiles?

Morgan eased up toward the first truck with

his M4 up and the weapon off safe. His finger wasn't on the trigger — the Marine Corps had beat it into his head to never do that until it was actually time to fire — but he was as close to shooting as a man in uniform could come.

He watched where he placed each foot. He only stepped on hard-packed dirt, but none of that would matter if these trucks were command-detonated. The one upside to command detonation was they might not waste the bombs on a single man. Unless they knew the bombs had been discovered.

Morgan had a plan for that. If he saw anything suspicious, he was going to play dumb and pretend not to have seen it. Then he would walk back to the MRAPs completely unconcerned. Tell the men to get up, pretend nothing was going on, and load up.

Once all the men were loaded, he'd get the MRAPs to back out of the square and then he'd order the last gunner to shred the trucks with their fifty until it exploded.

Not the best plan, but it might just work.

Sweat trickled into Morgan's right eye, stinging. And the weight of his "flak jacket," or modular tactical vest, was bulky and hot. With the ceramic plates in it, it would stop AK47 bullets, but the bitch weighed over 32 pounds.

That didn't count all the magazines, grenades, water, and other shit he was carrying, like radio, KA-BAR full-size fighting knife, first aid kit, and grenades.

Morgan felt like a slow-moving turtle. Got to be fast if the shit goes down, he told himself. Got to be fast.

It was something he always told himself. With so much gear, most men tend to let the weight slow them down. Morgan tried to avoid that feeling of lethargy.

He kept both eyes open, but one of them peered through the scope of M4 (the RCO, or Rifle Combat Optic). Morgan neared the first truck bed, then peered into its bed, keeping the barrel of his weapon aimed but out of reach of anyone who might be inside.

All the drama was for nothing. The bed was empty.

Morgan moved toward the truck cab. He watched each step, keeping an eye on where he placed his boots. His heart was beating so fast he felt it could explode any second. Who needed the Taliban when he was about a millisecond away from a heart attack?

The windows on the cab were up, as were the other trucks. That was incredibly strange in this oven-like hell hole. Why keep your windows up?

Morgan peered into the first cab, moving so that he could finally see through the glare.

Sayed Behzad's focus was locked on the man.

"Are the truck doors locked?" he snapped.

"I think so," his companion said.

"You don't sound certain," Behzad said. "You should have checked them."

The Marine pulled on the door handle and Behzad saw that it must be locked. He could almost see the frustration in the man's posture.

Would the man knock the window at? Apparently not. The man was walking up to the next truck, which he quickly checked.

"They're all empty," Behzad's companion said. The man was almost gleeful.

The Marine finished checking the fourth truck, and Behzad was almost relieved himself. But then he saw the Marine look at the open door across the square.

Morgan stood at the fourth truck, looking around. The trucks were empty, but each had been locked. Each had had their windows up.

What the hell was going on here? Why were there four trucks here? Four trucks that actually had windows still in them and looked just a few years old? Four trucks period? What kind of Afghan could afford those?

Morgan looked about. Something was going on, but he couldn't figure out what.

What do you need trucks for? Well, obviously to haul stuff. But hauling a bunch of men in the bed of white trucks was probably about the most stupid thing you could do in Helmand Province. It was a guaranteed way to attract attention from drones or aircraft.

Large groups of men would move by foot, ducking in wadi's or sneaking along mountain trails. Why trucks? And why leave them in the open, parked next to each other?

The answer hit him like a 2x4 to the head. Clearly these trucks were hauling something heavy. Like bomb-making material. And clearly they had been unloading something in the square when the two MRAPs showed up at Alim Nuaz

That was it. Then Morgan saw the door to the compound. Why were the trucks parked here? Because something had been carried into that room. That's why.

CHAPTER 18

The Gray Fox, Sayed Behzad, watched the Marine at the last truck, with the line of fighters laying behind him, and the two big armored MRAPs behind them. The Marine had finished searching the final truck.

The Marines had clearly been concerned there might be IEDs in the truck, but Behzad would never waste IEDs on some of the best trucks the Taliban owned in several hundred miles.

Plus, if the man had been thinking, he would have realized that the Taliban hadn't known this squad was coming, so there wasn't time to prepare IEDs for them in this instance.

"We may be all right," Behzad's companion said.

Behzad wanted to agree, but the old fighter held back. His left, useless arm started aching. He handed the binoculars to his companion, then used his good arm to pull his useless arm against his body. Behzad raised his eyes from the Marine and searched the sky above them.

Would this unit have a drone (or a couple of drones) circling them? Behzad rubbed his arm remembering the explosion, wondering yet again if it had been a drone or jet that bombed him and his friend Hafizullah.

His companion had seen his eyes.

"Our spotters report seeing no drones," the companion said. "I think these men are alone."

"You can't always see the drone," Behzad said.

His companion said nothing. How many times had Behzad said, "You can't always see the drone?" A couple dozen? A hundred?

The companion knew Behzad was a brave man, but he was terrified of drones and jets.

"Why is that Marine looking at the door? Behzad asked, using his right arm to reach for the pistol on his hip.

Immediately, a cold fear hit Behzad's companion.

It all made sense to Morgan. Four trucks, parked in an open area. Such a thing would draw the attention of any drones in the area. So why would the Taliban do it? Only a couple of reasons really.

The trucks were massive IEDs set up as a trap for some idiot like Morgan. But he had investigated them, and they weren't that. Their beds were empty and they weren't sitting low on their shocks from the weight of explosives.

That left the second reason: these trucks had

hauled something here. They had been used to transport something important and the Taliban had been caught by surprise. The unexpected patrol by the Marines had completely worked, and now Morgan wanted to exploit this find.

These trucks were parked here to be unloaded. And that door nearest them seemed the most pertinent place to look. Morgan turned behind him.

"My team, form up," he said. "We're going to see what's behind that door."

Sayed Behzad watched as the Marine near the trucks turned to his men, signaling toward the door.

"We can't allow them to get the missiles," Behzad said to his companion. "Call our fighters. We must run these men off before they find our stockpile."

"It will take a few minutes to get all the fighters back," the companion said. "They dispersed into the various huts, compounds, and tunnels."

"Then tell them to hurry!" Behzad snapped. "We can't lose those missiles."

Back in the plaza, Dean had jogged up next to Morgan.

"Where you want us, boss?" Dean asked.

"Take your four men and set up a perimeter in this square, covering the paths into it," Morgan said. "I'll take my boys and we'll see what's behind Door Number 1."

"This isn't a game show," Dean said. "That'd be a great place for an IED. They practically have a giant arrow pointed at it."

"They didn't have time to prepare for us," Morgan said. "And had no idea we'd be here. But nonetheless, I get your point. I'll be the first one in."

"Roger that," Dean said. He grabbed Morgan's shoulder and shook it a couple of times. "Be fucking careful. And check it out well before you open it."

CHAPTER 19

Sergeant Morgan's team of Hunt, Jordan, and Webb were stacked along the wall of the room Morgan wanted to enter. Behind them, in the fifty-yard-wide plaza, Dean's team of Anderson, Biggs, and Hernandez were formed in a loose perimeter, facing outboard in case danger came at them. The two big guns on the MRAPs were facing the deadly-looking openings of a couple of problematic-looking windows.

"We're set," Dean said over the radio.

"Roger," Morgan said. "We're entering."

He glanced down at his rifle and flexed his fingers on the pistol grip. He hated going through doors, like most of the men. You went from bright sunlight to pitch darkness. And you had no idea if there was a bomb on the door or five guys waiting inside with their weapons trained on the entrance.

Morgan switched the flashlight on the barrel of his rifle on. He glanced back at Hunt, Jordan, and Webb, stacked on the wall. Hunt, the motivator, would definitely follow him into the room if he entered it and shit hit the fan. Morgan was less certain about Jordan and Webb.

Enough dawdling, Morgan told himself, returning his attention to the door. A simple hasp lock with a padlock was all that was holding the door closed. But like most doors in the poorer provinces of Afghanistan, it was a half-hazard barrier at best.

The door frame of the mud hut wasn't even square and the door was handmade with planks of wood screwed together. Not like you'd screw boards together in America. These weren't laid together tightly and screwed flush with quality screws and tools. Instead, a half-hazard set of rusty screws were angled in from different directions with no seeming order.

Morgan figured a ten-year-old in America could have done a better job. But Afghan men weren't known for their building prowess. And they didn't have good tools. Boys in Afghanistan were taught how to handle a weapon or how to bury a perfectly-hidden IED over here; not use a screwdriver.

Morgan searched diligently for signs of a boobytrap, then set himself, reared back, and kicked with all his might. His thick boots drove the door inward and into three different pieces. One board hung by the lock, swinging like the pendulum of a grandfather clock.

Morgan shined the flashlight into the room,

saw nothing, and entered.

"Let's go," Morgan said over his shoulder.

He slid into the room, his flashlight hitting the corners and dead space of the corners. He hadn't really expected anyone to be inside because of the lock on the outside. Nonetheless, precautions had to be observed, and Hunt was on his shoulder, helping cover the danger areas.

But there was no need. The room was empty. It was a dry, mud-floored storage room, stacked with fiberglass cases. Actually, they looked like large, green suitcases. Heavy. Durable. Expensive. Something you pack weapons away in. Completely water and weatherproof.

"What the hell are those?" Hunt asked.

"I have no idea," Morgan said. He walked toward them.

"They may be booby-trapped," Hunt said, backing up. "Be careful."

"No way are these booby-trapped," Morgan said. He released his M4 and it dropped down across his chest thanks to his two-point, Viking Tactics combat sling. "The door was locked, the booby-traps would have been by the truck. These were hidden. Never expected to be found."

He walked over to them. His gut was screaming that he had just found the motherlode. What the hell were these things?

Morgan's radio squawked.

"We've got trouble coming," Dean said. "Enemy fighters approaching, and they're coming in a hurry."

Suddenly the sound of gunfire erupted outside the room, out in the plaza.

Morgan couldn't take his eyes off the suitcases.

"Hunt, get outside and take charge of the fireteam," Morgan said. "I have to see what's inside of these things."

Hunt exited and Morgan worked the latches on one of the cases. He lifted the lid, but in the darkness, he could barely make out the outline of a missile. He gasped. They were missiles. Olive drab. About three feet long. With controllers inside the cases.

Were these Soviet-made anti-tank missiles? He couldn't recall the name, but Morgan had read about the things in squad leaders course. But he'd never seen one of them in person. Having said that, though, he thought they *were* transported and stored in green cases somewhat similar to this.

What were they called? He couldn't remember.

Meanwhile, the firing outside increased in intensity. Morgan felt the pressure rise in his chest. He had to get outside, but he couldn't leave the things. How many were there? He counted. Twelve. Holy shit. Twelve of them.

"Man down," Dean said over the radio. "Morgan, you better get out here and do something."

"Fuck," Morgan yelled to himself.

Anderson, a Marine in Corporal Dean's fire-team, was in the kneeling position, using the corner of a compound wall for cover. He was looking down about a fifty-meter alleyway that ran between two compounds.

It was maybe four feet wide, with a small stream of what was probably water, piss, and shit running down the middle of it, away from the plaza. Thank goodness for small favors, Anderson thought.

He had a couple of thoughts running through his head. First, he was glad he had knee pads on because he felt like he'd been in this kneeling position for five minutes. He knew it hadn't been that long, but being in the infantry was hard as hell on the knees.

Anderson's second thought was that he was glad it wasn't his fireteam entering the room, or whatever the hell was behind the door that Sergeant Morgan was breaching. Going into a place like that was a great way to die, and Anderson had no plans to die any time soon.

It was bad enough being outside the building. He had had a bad feeling about the entire op. And that feeling had only grown worse. Entering Alim Nuaz with only eight men? That just struck Anderson as dumb as hell. Stupid in the extreme.

And he liked Morgan. Liked the man a lot. But sometimes, he was just too aggressive. Far too aggressive.

Come on, he said to himself. Hurry up, guys. The worst thing was that Anderson had been fighting a feeling of a terrible premonition. He just felt that something terrible was going to happen to him.

Why couldn't the first fireteam just enter the room, search it, and then get the whole squad the hell out of Alim Nuaz?

Anderson wanted to get back to Camp Leatherneck, eat some chow, and try to relax. A few of the Marines from Golf Company had a PlayStation set up. Anderson could handle playing some Grand Theft Auto.

A dog started barking in the distance. Others joined it. Anderson stopped daydreaming. He looked behind him into the plaza and saw what he already knew: he was alone as hell in this position. No Marine even near him for twenty yards.

Calm down, he told himself. You're a Marine. You're wearing a shitload of armor and have a freakin' M4. If anyone messes with you, they're going to die. Period. Just hold the position.

Anderson knocked away a fly that was buzzing his face when the impossible happened. A man came around the corner he was watching and before Anderson could even react, three more came running behind the man.

Four men, and holy shit, they were armed. Anderson had never seen a live Taliban fighter in Afghanistan. Usually, they fired from so far away that you might — if you were lucky — see dust

STAN R. MITCHELL

puffs from the firing of their rifles.

Here were four of them running toward him. Anderson was so startled that he hesitated on what to do at first. They hadn't seen him — the wall mostly hid him. Anderson freaked. He looked behind him, toward Dean and the rest of the men.

"Here come the Taliban," he yelled over his shoulder.

He looked back down the alley and saw the bearded, tall Taliban fighters stumbling and trying to stop their sprint down the alley. They were jabbering, looking for somewhere to go, and raising their weapons.

Anderson needed no more persuasion than that. It was kill or be killed, and his training finally kicked in.

He placed the red part of his scope on the first man and pulled the trigger. It was an easy shot. He could have hit the man with a pistol if he took his time. But the man didn't go down as Anderson expected. Hell, the rifle didn't even fire. And that's when Anderson remembered the weapon was on safe.

He flicked the weapon to fire and aimed again in a hurry. His target was bringing an AK up in what appeared to be slow motion. Time had slowed down, just as Anderson had always heard happened. The Taliban fighter — a severely tanned man who looked about fifty — was almost stable and halted from his running when Anderson's weapon kicked into his shoulder.

The Taliban fighter seemed to almost deflate. Like a spear had been driven through the man's midsection. Anderson's eyes relayed to his brain that the scope aperture had been low when the rifle fired and Anderson instantly aimed higher, pulling the trigger again.

The rifle bucked again and a second round entered the Taliban man, slapping into his chest and dropping him hard. The man was screaming and trying to drag himself along the ditch, back in the direction from which he had come, when Anderson fired into a second man.

That man had been aiming and in the process of firing when a bullet from Anderson shattered the man's forearm, careened off his rifle, and ricocheted back into the man's shoulder. It spun the man, and the man went to a knee. Before he could react better, Anderson fired again. This time, the scope had been on the man's head. And this time, the man dropped without a single convulsion.

This wasn't too hard, Anderson thought, as he moved his rifle to find one of the other two fighters. But they had stopped, leaned against opposite sides of the compound walls, and found Anderson in their own sights. They had iron sights, but it was basically spitting distance. Maybe thirty yards.

Their AK's blasted and rounds hit all around Anderson, hitting the wall, the ground all around his legs, and various parts of his body, including the body armor around his chest, his exposed shin, his shoulder, and part of his left hand, which had been supporting his M4 rifle. As he screamed and fell, he caught one thing scarier than even the victorious look of the two men still firing. They knew they were going to kill this American, who had taken two of their fellow brethren's lives. But even scarier than their cold, cruel grins was the line of men running behind them.

Anderson saw what had to be at least fifteen more men running behind them, and several of them had RPGs.

"We're all going to die," he thought. And with that thought, he screamed for help and dragged himself behind the corner of the mud wall as more rounds hit his legs and feet before he could retract them behind the wall.

CHAPTER 20

Corporal Dean watched as Anderson fired his rifle, but before Dean could sprint over to his man, a horde of bullets engulfed Anderson. The man went down, screamed, and crawled back behind the wall he was hiding behind.

Dean sprinted toward the corner.

"Biggs," Dean yelled. "Come with me."

The two Marines raced toward Anderson, who lay on his back, writhing in pain. Bullets raked the wall from where he had held his position. The Taliban were suppressing it, knowing that either Anderson or someone else would soon take up the position.

Dean and Biggs reached Anderson and they dragged him farther away from the wall. His uniform was painted in crimson in several places along the legs, and patches of red blood dotted the brown dirt from where he had lain.

"Patch him up," Dean said.

While Biggs broke out medical supplies, Dean peeked his head around the corner. A dozen fighters stood in the alleyway, two Taliban fighters were down, and several men were aiming toward him, protecting the group behind them.

Bullets slammed into the wall as Dean ducked back.

"Holy shit," he said. He saw Biggs pulling a tourniquet out. Good, he thought. Now to focus on the assholes around the corner. Dean yanked a grenade from a pouch, pulled the pin, counted to two, and hurled it around the corner.

The grenade exploded in an ear-piercing boom and screams of terror (and shrieks of pain) erupted from the alley.

"You fuckers like that?" Dean asked.

He was reaching for another grenade when an explosion boomed against the thick, mud wall he was hiding behind. The blast knocked him down and rattled his brain.

His slow-moving mind somehow made out what had happened. Those assholes fired an RPG into the wall, he thought. He checked himself for wounds but didn't see anything at first glance. Probably the shrapnel had gone into the wall or on past him since he was behind cover and it was a glancing, oblique shot.

Dean thumbed his radio.

"Man down," Dean said. "Morgan, you better get out here and do something."

Dean stuck his rifle barrel around the corner and for the first time in his life, he fired like an untrained Taliban fighter. He fired blindly around the corner, firing as fast as he could down the alley without looking over the sights of his rifle.

But return fire slammed into the wall and he had to yank his hands back. Blood covered both hands from pieces of rock and debris that bullets had thrown into his skin. Thankfully, he was wearing combat gloves or the injuries would have been much worse.

Dean turned.

"We've got to get the hell out of here!" he screamed to Biggs. "We're going to be overrun."

Dean reached down for Anderson, and Biggs helped him drag the shot-up man toward the two MRAPs. By now, the two MRAPs had focused their big guns on the danger area. As soon as the three Marines cleared the line of fire, they began engaging the corner with their big fifties. The roar and deafening rattle of the heavy machine guns would stop anyone from coming around that corner.

Sergeant Morgan left the room and ran across the square with his fireteam.

"How many are there?" he yelled to Dean.

"A ton," Dean answered. "Most I've ever seen. Has to be more than a dozen."

The two fifties continued suppressing the corner, using talking guns. One would fire: Ba-da. Ba-da. Ba-da. Then the other would fire. Ba-da. Ba-da. Ba-da. Ba-da. This kept the suppression constant and prevented either gun from overheating.

Morgan glanced down at Anderson on the

ground.

"How bad is he?" Morgan asked.

Dean shook his head no, signaling "not good."

But he said out loud, "He'll be fine. We just need to get him back in a hurry."

"I found missiles in that room," Morgan said. "You won't believe it. There's literally twelve wire-guided missiles in there."

"No way," Dean said, almost disbelieving. "Impossible."

An RPG roared into the square and exploded twenty meters beyond Morgan and Dean. They dove as the explosion rocked the area.

"Cover that window, Webb," Morgan said, pointing toward a dark window probably a hundred meters away.

Suddenly rounds started hitting the square, fired from behind them. A turret on an MRAP turned toward the new threat.

"We've gotta get out of here," Dean said. "They're going to overrun us."

The plaza was in a low area, with huts and buildings dominating it in each direction.

"This position isn't defensible," Dean said, reiterating his point.

"We have to load up the missiles," Morgan said.

Another RPG, fired from a new attack angle, roared into the square, barely missing an MRAP as everyone hit the deck again.

"We're surrounded," Dean said from the

ground. He lay near Morgan. "And we've got one seriously wounded. If we lose an MRAP, then none of us are getting out of here alive."

Morgan didn't want to agree, and he definitely didn't want to leave the missiles.

"We have to load those missiles," he said.

But then more bullets poured into the square from a fourth direction. Dean and Morgan fired toward them, but the truth was now obvious: the incoming fire was too much. They would soon take another casualty, for sure.

Morgan reluctantly ordered everyone to load up. The men shot and moved, working in pairs and retreating back to their vehicles. And as they withdrew, the firing at them grew heavier. But they managed to load Anderson into an MRAP and get everyone back to the relative safety of the armored vehicle without taking any more casualties.

"Get the hell out of here," Morgan said to his driver. The man needed no encouragement.

The two MRAPs left in a hurry, spinning around in the plaza and returning the way they had come. Their fifties fired bust-after-burst, trying to play whack a mole, but there were too many enemy fighters, firing from too many separate positions.

They were like two big dogs, surrounded by a swarm of yellow jackets. No matter how many they bit, more came. All the MRAPs could do was sprint away, no differently than two dogs. They had to get away from the proximity to the yellow jackets' nest.

CHAPTER 21

Sergeant Morgan stood in front of the desk of Captain Tomlin, aka "Godfather," aka company commander of Golf Company. To Morgan's right stood Lieutenant Flatt. Tomlin had his XO, standing next to Morgan as if she were no better than a private being ordered to report in. As if she wasn't his assistant and deputy, and worthy of a hundred times more respect.

Morgan stood there glaring at Tomlin and he had never hated the man more, but he knew he needed to be careful. He was covered in blood — Anderson's blood — and he was coming off the adrenaline surge that always followed combat.

Anderson was dead, had died before they could even get a helo out to him, and Morgan hated himself for the man's death.

But Tomlin was about to unleash holy hell on Morgan. And probably Flatt, too. Tomlin had wanted to see Morgan the moment he arrived back at base, but the battalion major had countered that order. Morgan had been told to go debrief the intelligence officer of the base first.

There, Morgan had been asked lots of questions. As had Hunt, who was the only other Marine that had entered the room and seen the missiles. They had been questioned separately: it was that big of a deal. No getting their stories together or influencing the other's words.

Morgan had repeatedly picked the missiles out of a stack of photos in a binder. Every time, his selection came up as AT-3 Sagger missiles. Hunt had picked the same thing. This was a big deal if it were true.

Two intel officers had tried to shake Morgan's confidence.

"These missiles aren't even in Afghanistan," a lieutenant colonel had said. "Look at the photos again of the missiles that are in theater, and quit making this up."

"How could I make this up?" Morgan said. "I hadn't seen those missiles since squad leader's course. I couldn't even remember their name. I'm not making this up."

Hunt had been just as confident, and the alarm bells were ringing all the way up the chain of command. Cobra helicopters had been dispatched to Alim Nuaz, but no trucks were in the area. Drones had been shifted as well, searching for any signs of where the trucks had gone, but they were nowhere to be found.

And no trucks meant that Morgan's story was even more suspect.

"Twelve of them?" the lieutenant colonel asked Morgan again. "Are you out of your mind?"

Morgan shrugged.

"That's how many cases there were," Morgan said. "I suppose some of them could have been empty."

"These things cost between thirty and fifty thousand dollars, and that's if you buy them in bulk from a supplier, such as Russia," the lieutenant colonel said. "On the black market, where these likely came from, they probably would cost a hundred thousand a piece. Do you really think the Taliban has one-point-two million dollars lying around? Fifteen plus years after we invaded and have destroyed most of their infrastructure and territory?"

"I'm just stating what I saw, sir," Morgan said. He was done with these asshole intelligence officers.

Morgan had suggested infantry units be redeployed around Alim Nuaz to find the missiles, but that had been laughed at. The Cobra helicopters had seen nothing, and not a single round had been fired at them. There weren't even any white flags flying above Alim Nuaz, Morgan had been told.

"Of course they're not," Morgan said. "The Taliban will want to keep a low profile until they finally decide to use them."

Morgan had been dismissed. All he wanted to do was get a shower, grab some food, and escape from it all. To process what had happened. But, no, Captain Asshole Tomlin had to get his licks in now.

"What the hell were you thinking?" Tomlin asked. "You go traipsing out all by yourself and get a Marine killed. What were you thinking?"

"I was thinking we could keep the enemy off guard, perhaps find some bomb-making caches, and maybe save some lives," Morgan said. "It's all in the patrol order that I filed."

"You killed a Marine," Tomlin screamed.

Morgan swallowed. This was going to be tougher than he had envisioned.

"Marines were dying before today," Morgan said. "We can't let the Taliban keep hitting us at their choice of timing and venue."

"You were sent here to protect my convoys," Tomlin said. "Now you've lost a man and can't even go out with us on the resupply convoy to-morrow."

Morgan nearly asked if Tomlin was going out on it, but he knew the captain wasn't. The man was glued to his chair and the safety of the massive walls around Camp Leatherneck these days.

Thankfully, Tomlin turned his attention to Flatt.

"Lieutenant Flatt, why did you not alert me to this foolish patrol?" he asked.

Flatt bristled at the question.

"Sir, in the past, when I told you about the operations that Sergeant Morgan was undertaking, you expressed little interest. In fact, you dismissed me several times and said you didn't want to hear about it."

"They weren't going into Alim Nuaz on those patrols!" he screamed. "This was a major endeavor! You don't think I wanted to know?"

Flatt said, "Understood, sir," which was probably the only thing she could say, Morgan figured.

Morgan was glad Dean wasn't here. Dean would have probably knocked Tomlin's teeth down his goddamn throat.

"Sir," Morgan said, "we were having very little success guarding the convoys by simply tagging along in the pack. Never even deploying. These patrols have shown that they have kept the Taliban off guard. And today, we nearly seized twelve highly-valuable weapons from the enemy."

"I'm not buying that those weapons are in-country," Tomlin snapped. "I'm not buying that you saw them. You came up with that story so that the death of your Marine wouldn't seem such a waste. And I'm sure you convinced Hunt, your most loyal man, to corroborate your story."

Morgan couldn't stand being called a liar, but the man had a lot of rank on his collar, so he kept his mouth shut. For now.

"We're clearly not getting anywhere," Tomlin said. "Both of you get out of my office. We'll finish this later."

Morgan and Flatt left without another word.

CHAPTER 22

The next day, Sergeant Morgan stood by Lieutenant Flatt. It was gray light of dawn and all the trucks in the convoy were already running, their loud diesel motors drowning out what should have been the peace of morning.

"I can't believe you all are going out," Morgan said. "If the Taliban uses those missiles on your convoy, you'll be sitting ducks. They can literally fire at a distance beyond the range of your fifties or Mark 19s."

"They don't believe you, remember?" Flatt said.

"I know what I saw," Morgan said. "And I know how hard the Taliban came at us. They were protecting something. Something big."

"I believe you," Flatt said. "But supplies have to be delivered, and you're not the only one who gets to be brave out here partner."

She patted his chest and it felt good. They had grown fairly close. As close as possible, given their differences in rank.

Sayed Behzad watched the convoy of heavy trucks and armored vehicles as it moved through the valley. Eighteen vehicles. Moving as slow as a line of turtles crawling across the desert floor. In many ways, this was the perfect analogy.

The trucks were protected by machine guns, much as a turtle was protected by its hard shell. Just as turtles had little to fear, the trucks had such incredible firepower on them that the Taliban were usually scared to take them on. The trucks were teaming with weapons. Fifty caliber machine guns. Forty-millimeter grenade launchers. 7.62 medium machine guns.

The convoys were quite fierce. Much better to hit them with IEDs than try to take them on.

But today would be different. Today would be *much* different.

Behzad's men would be hitting the convoy from the ridgelines that lined both sides of the valley, and the Taliban serving under Behzad would be firing from more than 2,500 meters away. Far outside the range of the Americans.

Behzad knew the limitations of every gun on the American convoy. The fifty-cal machine guns could only fire accurately roughly 1,800 meters. The forty-millimeter grenade launchers: 1,500 meters. Behzad's missiles: 2,500 meters.

Simple math. It wouldn't be a fair fight. The convoy would be as helpless as a turtle smashed by a man swinging a heavy sledgehammer. In short, the convoy couldn't even move fast enough to get away.

Behzad smiled, imagining the aftermath. Today, Sayed Behzad would finally make a name for himself. Today, he would avenge the Americans for the missile strike that permanently damaged his left hand and killed his best friend Hafizullah.

He used his good right hand to pull up the M9 Beretta he carried as his personal weapon of choice. A pistol was mostly useless in most firefights, but on this day, with luck, he might get to use it against some wounded American.

If he were truly lucky, they could capture one of the Marines and he could film a propaganda video with Behzad standing behind the man. And after a few remarks, Behzad could use the pistol on the man.

It wouldn't be as good as a proper beheading video, but you couldn't behead an American with a sword when you only had one good hand. He cursed the Americans again for their missiles and drones.

Today, he would get his vengeance. He lifted his radio.

"Convoy has entered the kill zone," Behzad said on the radio. "Gunners, prepare to launch on my command."

Lieutenant Flatt had no inclination of the attack until it happened. Her convoy had just entered the village of Gorahumbira. Captain Tomlin had stayed at Camp Leatherneck, true to form.

In many ways, she was glad he had. She despised him, and she hated the foolish command decisions he made. Back at Leatherneck, Tomlin's chances of getting folks killed were lower.

Flatt returned her focus to the task at hand. The town of Gorahumbira was a dangerous place. Not as dangerous as Alim Nuaz, but it was no laughing matter either.

White Taliban flags stood proudly on long wooden poles at the corners of several compounds in the town. They're literally flaunting their hatred of us, and their support of the Taliban, she thought. And America back home thinks we're winning out here.

Focus, she told herself.

"Truck 1, is it still clear up there?" she asked.

"So far, so good," her sergeant in the lead vehicle reported.

Sayed Behzad screamed into the air, "Allahu Akbar! Allahu Akbar!" The phrase meant "God is great," a very common phrase among Muslims.

Behzad wasn't worried about the Americans hearing him. He was more than 2,000 meters away. Back with one flank of his missile gunners. The line of missiles was on the far ridge.

He had carefully selected this ambush site. A wide valley, almost perfectly five thousand meters wide. It had high ground on both sides, from which his men could launch the missiles. It was almost as though Allah himself had designed this valley for the slaughter that was about to take place.

And Behzad knew that indeed, Allah had. Allah had placed the informant inside Camp Leatherneck, who worked as a general laborer and regularly provided updates on when convoys would be rolling out. Allah had provided the missiles from Iran, which were now in their possession. And Allah had spared Behzad's life when the missile fell from the sky, which had killed his friend Hafizullah.

With his prayer over, as well as his moment of gratitude, Behzad lifted his radio once more.

"Gunners, launch your missiles. And may Allah grant us the strength to kill all the infidels in this valley."

CHAPTER 23

Lieutenant Flatt knew as the first moments of horror struck her convoy that if she were lucky enough to survive the ordeal, she'd never forget each and every moment that passed in the next moments of her life. No matter how long she lived. She knew this was going to be life-changing even before it fully occurred.

It was that feeling you had in a horrendous car crash, in that millisecond before it all goes down. One moment, you're doing sixty-five. You're half-awake, and certainly not alert. Just another day on the road. The next moment, the car is losing traction. And time just slows. And there, deep in your gut, you know. You know you're going to get hurt so bad that you'd give just anything to back up the clock ten seconds and slow that car down dramatically.

Flatt knew she was in trouble the moment it all began because her convoy was perfectly split up into three separate groups. The front end of the column was out-of-sight, having just entered a small town. The rear of the column was around the bend, but it might as well have been ten miles away. The bottom line was that you couldn't have selected a better spot to ambush them.

Flatt's first inclination that something was wrong was an explosion that shook her MRAP. At first, she thought IED. But the results weren't like those that happened after an IED, which had basically become routine.

Screams came into the radio.

"Oh my God, help us!! Help us!! We're on fire! Oh, God, please help us!!"

Before she could do a thing, more explosions followed. BOOM. BOOM. BOOM-BOOM. BOOM.

The radio was filled with Marines shrieking, crying, begging for help.

"Open the fucking hatch," she said, before running out the back of her MRAP. She had to figure out what was going on. Why were so many MRAPs being hit? And just what the hell was hitting them? Was it mortars?

BOOM. BOOM.

More explosions kept happening, and then something exploded into the side of her own MRAP, throwing her to the ground and nearly blowing out her eardrums. She tried to stabilize herself and raise up, but her head — and entire world — was spinning.

Marines were screaming from her MRAP. Marines were screaming on the radio. Her ears were ringing so loud that she could barely make it out.

She looked to the front of the convoy and saw vehicle-after-vehicle on fire. Flames roaring. Smoke rising. Marines staggering out of vehicles, holding bloody limbs and wounded comrades. She looked to the rear of the convoy. Same scene.

Two more explosions happened, and then it all stopped. Just like that.

"Medic! Medic!" someone screamed into the radio.

Other Marines were yelling toward her — not using the radio — saying the same thing. "We need a medic, lieutenant! We need a medic!"

Flatt stared to the left, and its daunting ridgeline, and then to the right, where another ridgeline stood. She couldn't see anyone, but the distances were so great. Had it been missiles? Were the attacks over? Or did the enemy have more missiles?

She needed to call Camp Leatherneck. Immediately.

She ran to the back of her MRAP to grab her radioman. He should have been following her, anyway. He knew the rules. Where the hell was he?

She peered back into the MRAP and saw it was filled with smoke. She ran into it. Flames burned and popped. Bodies lay shredded and charred. She couldn't tell who was whom in the darkness, so she started dragging Marines out as fast as she could, without even taking the time to see who was dead or alive.

When the first body was out, she screamed

into her radio, "I can't find the company radio. Someone alert Camp Leatherneck that we've been hit, have lots of wounded, and need all the support we can get. Air support. Ground troops. Medical EVACs. Everything."

She knew she sounded hysterical. And with the way her ears were ringing, she had probably been yelling too loud. But what else could she do?

She ran into the MRAP to drag more Marines out. How many had been in her vehicle? She couldn't remember. Three? Four? Her head was so fuzzy, and moving so slow. So very slow. Did she have a concussion, too?

Someone on the radio said, "I've got a message sent up on the net. We'll get some help here soon." Sending two-way text messages was one of the main ways the convoy communicated with Camp Leatherneck. The messages traveled by satellite. Good, she thought.

Flatt knew she needed to get near a radio fast so she could get better information sent into Leatherneck. They'd soon be flooding her with messages. But first, she needed to drag the rest of the Marines out of her MRAP.

"First Sergeant," she yelled into her radio, "I need an update on casualties. All gunners, be on the alert. All riflemen, be ready for an attack. This may not be over."

Flatt, staggering about from the effects of the explosion, had no idea how right she was.

CHAPTER 24

Sayed Behzad watched the explosions through a pair of binoculars. Enemy vehicle after enemy vehicle exploded. His gunners were on top of their game on this day. They had listened well to their Iranian trainer and even surpassed the typical statistical average because only two missiles had missed their mark.

"Allahu Akbar!" Behzad screamed.

God is great.

After a moment of celebration, Behzad ordered forward the second part of his operation. He had held his main body of troops back in reserve. It was crucial that the men, and the four white trucks that they had, remain hidden. Only the missile gunners were allowed to be visible, and they were to stay as hidden as possible.

Behzad hadn't wanted to give away the ambush to alert Marines in the convoy prior to the ambush. But with the ambush launched, his main attack from the flank could truly begin.

"Behead the infidels," he said into his radio.

Men cheering came back on the radios, as commanders acknowledged the orders.

Let them cheer, Behzad thought. They had just witnessed a tremendous victory for Allah and the Afghan people. Now, it was time for them to contribute their part.

Things were still incredibly hectic at the convoy. Lieutenant Flatt was doing her best to reorganize her unit. Typically, the standard operating procedure was to push through ambushes, and not allow the enemy to get you to stop under any circumstances.

But this was no ordinary circumstance. Seven MRAPs were out of commission. They weren't drivable, period. Three others *were* drivable, but the missiles had killed or wounded most of the occupants. Flatt's First Sergeant, and several staff sergeants, were trying to gather the men into groups for aid, as well as count the killed or wounded.

But things remained too hectic and out of control. The convoy was too strung out, Flatt thought, and too many Marines helped wounded men instead of looking outboard for threats. Camp Leatherneck was both calling and texting for updates. Updates that Flatt couldn't provide, because she still didn't know what the hell had happened to her unit.

No incoming fire was happening. The convoy had simply been hit with a shit-load of missiles —

or something. And then silence.

Nothing like this had ever happened before. Of that, she was certain.

Air assets were being diverted, but they wouldn't arrive for at least a half-hour. The only good news was medical evacs were warming up to leave Leatherneck. Perhaps some of the critically injured could still be saved.

Her battalion commander back at Leatherneck was screaming for target grids to hit with artillery, but she nor none of her Marines had any idea of the enemy's location. She could request both hillsides be hit, but that was miles of ground — both horizontally and vertically — and with no clear targets, her request would be denied. Leatherneck wanted precise targets. Not some wide area where kids could be playing.

Flatt felt almost completely overwhelmed with the situation. And that's when the Taliban struck again.

CHAPTER 25

Sayed Behzad had scouted out a route from the hillside down to the convoy. His trucks would traverse this pre-selected path. Every part of the fight had been rehearsed for days.

Behzad smiled at fate.

The Americans had gotten close to grabbing his precious missiles, and he had lost many good men defending them, but it was worth it. Watching so many smoking vehicles down in the valley and imagining all the dying Marines writhing in pain, Behzad shouted, "Allahu Akbar!" again.

This victory would stand up there with Mogadishu, Somalia. With the attack on the U.S.S. Cole. With the bombings of the two African embassies. Behzad, the Gray Fox, had scored a victory that would cement his name in history.

He would send a bonus payment to his informant at Camp Leatherneck. He picked up his binoculars to watch his trucks as they sped toward the convoy.

Lieutenant Flatt still didn't have things under

control. She glanced toward the town in front of her. It was probably five hundred meters from her vehicle. And she knew at least three vehicles remained inside the town of Gorahumbira.

They were out of sight, and so far, they hadn't been attacked. That was the good news. The bad news was they couldn't turn around. And the road they were on was so narrow that backing up all three MRAPs was going to take some time.

Nonetheless, she had ordered them to do so.

Flatt looked behind her. Numerous MRAPs continued to burn, as Marines ran around providing aid to Marines or pulling wounded men from vehicles. Other Marines ran from vehicle to vehicle. These were senior enlisted men. Staff sergeants and her First Sergeant, trying to determine how many men were wounded or KIA.

The worst problem — besides having so many dead and wounded, and having three MRAPs stuck in the town of Gorahumbira — was that she couldn't see the vehicles farther back in the column. There was a curve around a small hill and the MRAPs were farther out of sight.

Her battalion commander had asked her on the radio what was the main problem, other than needing air support and medical evacs. It had seemed such a foolish question, but suddenly she realized what the main problem was: her force was separated into three distinct groups.

Three untouched and powerful MRAPs were stuck inside Gorahumbira, where they were useless. The middle of her convoy was busted-up, shot to hell, and full of wounded. And the rear of her column was useless, unable to provide any support to the decimated center.

Well, she could at least fix part of her problems.

"All vehicles in the rear, move forward and consolidate with the center," she said.

Vehicle commanders acknowledged the order and she felt just the first sense of relief and control return. And that's when she heard these heart-stopping words on the radio: "Here they come!! Taliban vehicles approaching from the left flank!"

CHAPTER 26

Back at Camp Leatherneck, Sergeant Grant Morgan and Corporal Sam Dean heard about the attacks on Lieutenant Flatt's convoy almost as soon as they happened. A sergeant, whom they had bonded with inside the command center, sent a runner to their quarters moments after the sergeant realized the gravity of the situation.

Morgan and Dean looked up as the man entered. The man was winded and out of breath. Morgan and Dean had been playing a game of Poker on Dean's cot. Wasn't like there was much else they could do at the moment.

"Sergeant Dobbs sent me," the PFC said, huffing, "to tell you that you better get your squad ready. The Golf Company convoy has been hit hard."

"What happened?" Morgan asked as he and Dean dropped their hands of cards.

"I'm not sure," the PFC said, still trying to catch his breath. "He just told me to give you a heads up."

"Thanks," Morgan said, reaching for his M4. "Tell him we really appreciate that."

Morgan and Dean, who were wearing pants, boots, and t-shirts, threw on their blouses and covers. They grabbed their weapons and raced down to the command center, yelling at Marines to get out of their way. Their commotion alerted everyone in their path that some kind of attack or terrible event had occurred.

Marines only sprinted at Camp Leatherneck when bad shit had gone down.

A few Marines said silent prayers for what they felt certain were fallen comrades. One yelled out, "Yut! Get some!" Another said, "Fuck rushing around like that for *any* body. Especially some pogue-ass officer or lifer staff NCO."

Morgan and Dean ignored all comments, and they didn't slow until they arrived — out of breath, as well — at the command center, which was more than half a mile away.

Almost no one looked up as they burst into the room. A captain and several others completely ignored them; they had more pressing matters, including the battalion commander, who was screaming into a radio in one hand, and pointing at a map and demanding information from the captain and other officers with the other.

Morgan and Dean had been in the command center during many IEDs and situations, where Marines were wounded. Most of the time, it was calm; men were under control and making things happen.

This was something completely different. This was a, "Houston, we have a problem" situation.

Sergeant Dobbs broke away and rushed up to them.

"Shit has hit the fan," Dobbs said. "Flatt's convoy was hit with multiple missiles. We think wire-guided."

"I knew it," Morgan said.

"How many wounded or killed?" Dean asked.

"We have no idea," Dobbs said. "But for sure a fuck ton. Probably thirty or more."

Morgan and Dean looked at each other. That seemed impossible.

"We've got to get there," Dean said, saying precisely what Morgan was thinking.

They exited the command post in a jog, running into Hunt — ever the motivated Marine — who was waiting outside the door in the hallway.

"What's going on?" Hunt asked.

"Too much to tell," Morgan said. "The Taliban knocked the hell out of Flatt and Golf Company. Tell the squad to suit up and be ready to go. We're going in."

"Roger that," Hunt said. He turned and raced back to their quarters. Morgan and Dean ran the opposite direction, toward Captain Tomlin's office.

They'd have to get approval to leave Camp Leatherneck, and that meant getting Tomlin to sign off on it.

"If that motherfucker doesn't let us go," Dean said, as they neared the man's office.

Morgan didn't need to reply. He was as worried about Tomlin saying "no" as Dean was.

CHAPTER 27

Lieutenant Flatt couldn't believe her ears. Taliban vehicles approaching from the right flank? That was impossible.

The Taliban had never attacked a convoy with trucks. Not that she had heard of. It would be suicide against the fifties and Mark 19s on the MRAPs.

"Say again," she said into the radio, looking toward the left flank.

A dust cloud was indeed rising toward them, with vehicles or something moving quickly. And then she saw a white truck, followed by other white trucks bursting out of the dust, racing toward them. Probably moving thirty miles per hour.

Well-armed fighters stood in the backs of the trucks, holding on for now. But soon, they'd be rushing the perimeter. Except, the Marines had no perimeter for the moment.

"Light them up!" she screamed into the radio.

And then she looked up and down the line of vehicles near her and saw that none of the turrets were occupied. Some were still smoking from the missile strikes. Others had been abandoned so that every hand on deck could help do triage on all the wounded.

"No!" she screamed, mostly to herself and not pushing the radio button. What had already been the absolute worst day of her life was about to get a whole lot worse.

She snapped her M4 off safe and ran toward the center of the line where the trucks were heading.

"Get on the guns!" she screamed into the radio. "Someone get on the guns and form up a line of riflemen on the left flank. Do it now!"

Some Marines were starting to respond, ignoring the wounded who were laid out on the ground, but it was going to be too late. She could see that. It was going to be way too late. The trucks were within five hundred meters and spreading out from a single column into a wide line that looked completely unstoppable.

CHAPTER 28

Back at Camp Leatherneck, Captain Tomlin said, "Absolutely not. You guys are not going out there. No siree."

"Marines are dying," Sergeant Morgan said again.

"We are not some infantry company," Tomlin said, "who goes running off toward the sound of guns. We are a logistics company. And right now, our logistical priority is to recover a bunch of shot-up, half-destroyed MRAPs. Your squad will be a part of that recovery convoy. We're trying to assemble a convoy with several wreckers and flatbeds to load the disabled vehicles on. We need your men to protect it."

"We can help with that once they arrive," Morgan said, "but surely it will take hours to get the convoy ready, and then even more time to arrive at Lieutenant Flatt's position. Marines are bleeding out and dying as we speak. They could use our squad out there."

"I'm not arguing with some lowly sergeant,"

Tomlin said. "Especially one who's not even spent six months in a logistics company. You don't know how we operate. I might listen to my First Sergeant's counsel, but the man has spent twenty years in logistics. You two are dismissed. I'm not arguing with you anymore."

"What the fuck, sir?" Dean said.

Tomlin looked up, enraged.

"What did you just say?" Tomlin asked. "I'll have your ass for that. And at least one stripe."

"You can have both my stripes," Dean said, "you fucking pogue-ass bitch."

Morgan grabbed Dean and yanked him toward the door.

"I'll handle this," Morgan said, looking back.

"No, you won't," Tomlin said. "That man will be officially charged, reprimanded, and court-martialed. And I'll have your ass, too. Get back here, Morgan."

Morgan pretended not to hear, slamming the door behind him.

"Let's go," he said to Dean. "We better haul ass before fatass gets around his desk."

They ran down the corridor, past several headquarters staff who looked up too slowly, as the shouts of the captain echoed behind them.

"That motherfucker," Dean said.

Once they had gotten away, several buildings away, Dean asked, "Are you thinking what I'm thinking?"

Morgan said, "I am indeed. I'm not sitting on

base while Marines are dying out there."

"I'm not either," Dean said. "Let's grab our gear and get in the shit."

"We're fucked no matter what," Morgan said. "Might as well go down doing what real Marines do."

CHAPTER 29

Lieutenant Flatt raised her M4, peering through her scope. The four trucks were closing so fast. Not at the speed one would expect trucks to drive in America. Not sixty or eighty miles per hour. But this was Afghanistan, where any truck traffic was at a crawl unless on a paved road; and paved roads basically didn't exist in Helmand Province.

Yet these trucks were hauling ass. Easily forty miles per hour. And as she aligned the center truck in her scope, it occurred to her that these bastards had studied the terrain ahead of time. They had known their approach route. Was there anything they hadn't already planned out? The thought brought chills.

But she pulled the trigger and fired her first round. The Taliban were firing, as well, sending rounds toward the Marines from the back of the trucks. The rounds weren't particularly accurate, zipping overhead and into the dirt, and Flatt ignored the shots. They were a distraction.

There was no way the Taliban could hit anything they were aiming at from the back of the truck. Hell, the Taliban could barely hit what they were aiming at when they *weren't* bouncing around.

Flatt couldn't tell where her first round had hit, but she dropped to a knee to make her aim more steady. She began firing on single shot — BAM, BAM, BAM, BAM, BAM — and her shots were making impacts. Hitting the truck's grill, the front windshield, the front windshield again, and then smashing into a fighter she aimed at after realizing her bullets might be glancing off the angled windshield.

The man dropped, and she fired hastily at the man next to him. She jerked the trigger on that shot, missing badly. She wanted to kick herself for that.

Marines don't miss, she told herself.

Flatt was aiming at another fighter when something knocked her to the ground.

The trucks had closed to one hundred meters and almost no return fire was coming from the Marine convoy. Flatt had been one of the last firing.

Sayed Behzad watched as his fighters closed the final distance to the convoys. As expected, the Marines returned a ferocious volley of deadly fire. There weren't many of them. Maybe just eight or nine total, who weren't already wounded or killed. And the front of the column and the rear of the column was still out of sight.

But even with just eight or nine Marines firing, it might be enough. For a moment, he thought the Marines might just stop them. He felt fear rise up. So much was on the line. So much planning. So much preparation. Everything he had put together to not only build his own name up but to also advance the cause of the Taliban. And to advance the name of Allah, of course. He scolded himself for forgetting the true motivations of his efforts.

Allah might have been blessing their efforts, but Behzad's faith faltered as the Marines killed more of his men. The enemy was renowned for their marksmanship and Behzad cringed to imagine how many of his men were being killed in the return fire.

Where were the snipers?

And then, praise be to Allah, his hidden fighters emerged. Or, Behzad assumed they did. He couldn't see them. They were extremely well-concealed in prepared hides, and they had been trained by snipers in Pakistan, who themselves had been trained by the Americans.

There was a deep irony in this fact, but America mostly saw Pakistan as an ally, so it continued to help train Pakistan's fighters. Pakistan played a shrewd hand, pretending to remain America's ally while also protecting and overlooking the activities of the religious madrassas (or schools).

But back to the matter at hand, there was no way Behzad could see the men from so high up. Yet he knew they were now involved in the fight. Because Marines started getting knocked down.

Behzad had four fighters in hides dug into the ground. At less than three hundred meters away, his men couldn't miss. They were firing 7.62 Dragunov sniper rifles, with four-power scopes. At anything within eight hundred meters, his men wouldn't be missing.

Behzad watched as Marine-after-Marine was dropped by his snipers.

He smiled. It was finished. His trucks pulled alongside the MRAPs, deploying in a half-circle. Taliban fighters dismounted and ran among the bodies.

They had a single goal: find a Marine still alive, if at all possible.

Behzad planned to execute the Marine on video. It would be similar to the beheadings done by ISIS. And it would do so much for the cause. For the Taliban. For the march onward of Islam.

Soon, he thought. Soon.

CHAPTER 30

As Morgan and Dean ran to their quarters, where the squad was waiting, they could hear the sound of helicopters winding up their enormous engines, the rumble roaring louder and louder. The helicopters had been called out to the convoy to pick up seriously wounded Marines. Morgan and Dean intended to catch a ride with them to the ambush site.

"We better hurry," Dean said.

They kicked it into high gear, sprinting as fast as they could. Behind them, the noise of the choppers increased.

They burst into their squad bay, where their two fireteams were gearing up. The urgent entrance of the two team leaders silenced the room. Their men were gearing up, but nowhere near as quickly — or serious — as their NCOs. It was as if they knew Captain Tomlin wouldn't have them moving any time soon.

"We leaving that quickly?" Jordan asked, standing.

"No," Morgan said, slinging his assault vest, armor, and helmet on. His speed suggested Camp Leatherneck was about to fall to some kind of impending attack.

"What's going on, Sergeant?" Webb asked.

"Everyone, shut up with the questions," Dean said. "You'll find out soon enough."

"Hunt, come with me," Morgan said, as he and Dean rushed out of the room, running with all their gear in their arms. Behind them, Hunt ran as fast as he could to catch up.

"Do I need my gear?" Hunt asked. He didn't have his pack.

"No," Morgan said. "Just keep up."

As the two NCOs sprinted toward the helo's, pulling on straps and snapping on gear, Hunt caught up. He wasn't burdened down with nearly as much weight, after all.

"What's going on?" Hunt asked.

"Just listen," Morgan said. "Dean and I are heading out to reinforce Lieutenant Flatt. Captain Tomlin said our squad would be used to protect a convoy of vehicles that will have several wreckers and trailers to pick up disabled MRAPs."

"What do I—"

"Shut up!" Dean said, filling in for Morgan. "You're in charge of the squad. Get them ready, and if necessary, lead them on the recovery convoy. Most likely, we'll be back before that happens, but take charge if we're not."

Hunt started to say, "Aye, aye," but his words

would have been useless.

The sound of two CH-53s helicopters was so loud that words were useless. The choppers were practically lifting off when Morgan and Dean raced up the ramp.

"What the hell?" the crew chief asked, holding out his hand to stop them.

"We're going with you," Morgan yelled above the roar of the motor.

"You're not on the manifest," the crew chief said.

"Fuck your manifest," Dean said, getting in the man's face. "Captain Tomlin ordered us on this bird. If you want to waste five minutes discussing with him this screw-up while Marines are bleeding out in the field, be my guest. But I'm betting he'll court-martial your ass for doing so."

"What's going on back there?" the pilot asked into the radio.

At least that's what Morgan figured the man asked, because the crew chief said, "These two Marines are saying Captain Tomlin ordered them on the bird. But they're not on our manifest, sir."

The officer responded with something, and the crew chief replied, "Yes, sir."

"Take a seat," the crew chief said. "We're lifting off."

Dean could barely contain his shit-eating grin as they sat down, turned their weapons muzzle down, and buckled in.

CHAPTER 31

The Taliban fighters moved amongst the wounded Marines. Most, who wouldn't last but a few minutes anyway, were executed. Single shots, right to the head. A Taliban fighter recorded the entire scene. This footage alone was priceless.

It was like a movie: Taliban fighters screaming, "Allahu Akbar!" Firing their weapons in the air. Executing wounded Marines as if it were the easiest thing in the world.

The Taliban fighters found two Marines who looked like good candidates for Sayed Behzad's purpose. One had a badly wounded lower arm. The other, a shredded lower leg. But both would live probably an hour or two. Especially since both had tourniquets already applied.

The two Marines didn't have weapons nearby, but they still tried to stand and fight. But it was a lost cause. They were beaten into submission with rifle stocks until they lay on the ground helpless. The Taliban removed their armor and gear. Taliban fighters taped their hands behind their back, and then the two men were tossed without much care into the rear of two trucks.

The roar of approaching motors from the south caused the Taliban to realize they better get a move on.

"More trucks are coming," a Taliban fighter said, as he ran up from where the rear of the column remained.

"Load up," one of the leaders in the trucks said.

The men were running back to the trucks when they saw a Marine, who had been motionless on the ground, move. They had thought the Marine dead. After all, the Marine's helmet had a bullet hole in it. Blood had flowed down the Marine's neck and into the dirt.

But the body was moving.

"Check him out," the leader said.

A Taliban fighter ran over, pushed the body to his back, and nearly died at what he saw. It was a female, and she was very much alive. The bullet had only barely impacted her head. It must have simply knocked her out, after losing most of its force penetrating the helmet.

"Grab her!" the leader said.

The two CH-53 helo's were nearly on station when the crew chief jogged up to Morgan and Dean.

"For a minute there, we thought we might have to circle back," the crew chief said. "The Taliban breached the Marine perimeter."

"They did what?" Morgan asked. "That's impossible."

"We thought so, too," the crew chief said, "but drone footage confirmed it. But the rear of the column has pushed forward and linked up, securing the perimeter. I don't know what you boys are dropping into, but it's a hell of a situation."

"Just get us there," Morgan said. "Two more shooters on the ground are bound to help."

The CH-53s dropped down and landed opposite of where the Taliban trucks had come from. That was presumed to be the safest location, since the convoy still hadn't realized that it had been attacked from two directions.

Morgan and Dean ran off the back of the 53, fighting the wind blasts off the two humongous birds. Marines were running toward the choppers, carrying emergency stretchers.

Morgan and Dean ran past the Marines and their wounded, never slowing down. This was really bad. Morgan counted fifteen Marines on stretchers.

One man appeared to be in charge, pointing and shouting.

"Head that way," Morgan said, pointing toward him.

Dean altered his course and the two of them ran up to him.

"What the hell are you all doing here?" the company first sergeant asked.

"I think there was some confusion back at Leatherneck on whether we were supposed to come out or not," Dean said, keeping a straight face.

The first sergeant studied Dean's face, then looked at Morgan's.

"Sure," he said. "The captain will have your ass for this."

Morgan shrugged.

"We don't care," he said. "Give us a quick sitrep. Was that really fifteen seriously wounded I just saw loaded onto the birds?"

The Marines who had carried the wounded were running back with empty stretchers.

"Yeah," the first sergeant said. "Fifteen seriously wounded. And twelve KIA."

"Twelve KIA?!" Dean asked, incredulously. "There's no way. The Corps hasn't lost that many Marines in a single day since the war started. Since probably Beirut in '83."

The Corps had lost 241 Marines in a twin truck-bombing attack, back in 1983 when Reagan was president.

"You didn't let me finish," the first sergeant said. He spat toward the ground. "We've got three MIA."

"You've got what?" Morgan asked.

"Well, they're not MIA," the first sergeant said. "They were captured. The Taliban drove four white trucks up, executed quite a few wounded, and then captured three Marines, who they took with them."

"White trucks?" Dean asked.

"Yep," the first sergeant said.

"We've seen those before," Dean replied.

"Which way did they go?" Morgan asked.

"Toward that mountain," the first sergeant said, gesturing toward the hill. "I'm still trying to get a decent perimeter set up, but command back at Leatherneck isn't authorizing any kind of rescue party to try to find them. They're still afraid we're going to be hit and possibly overrun, like we were before."

"Do they at least have a rescue party on the way?" Morgan asked.

"There's not squat for responding forces anywhere near us," the first sergeant said. "Remember, all the fighting is many hours south. And even down there, the battalion is all spread out and engaged in various ops. We'll be lucky if *any* troops make it here before dark."

Neither Morgan nor Dean said anything.

"They're telling me," the first sergeant said, "that it will be at least five hours before any ground forces can arrive. And that's if we're lucky."

Morgan looked out toward the mountain.

"We can't allow that," he said.

"You thinking what I'm thinking?" Dean asked.

It never ceased to amaze Morgan how Dean seemed to always be on the exact same page as him.

The first sergeant said, "There's no way I'm letting you all take an MRAP to go after them. We've

barely got eight of them that are even undam-
aged."

"We wouldn't need an MRAP," Morgan said.

"Did you miss the part where I said the Taliban
were in four trucks?" the first sergeant asked.

Morgan didn't say anything, and Dean had for
once sealed his own lips.

"I'm not sure what you maniacs are thinking,"
the first sergeant, "but it's probably best if I don't
hear it."

"It definitely is," Morgan said. "You walk away
and we'll leave instructions with some other NCO.
Besides, you've got enough on your plate already
with the wounded, setting up a better defense,
and managing responding air power."

The first sergeant said, "There will soon be
enough air power in this valley that the Taliban
won't be able to pass gas without us knowing. But
it's still a good hour away."

"Lieutenant Flatt directing it?" Morgan asked.

"No," the first sergeant said, looking at him
strangely. "You didn't hear? She's one of the
Marines the Taliban nabbed."

"Then my decision is made," Dean said.

"You better walk away," Morgan said to the
first sergeant. "Don't trash your career along with
us. We haven't put in nearly as long."

The first sergeant gave a knowing nod, clasped
both Morgan and Dean on the shoulders, and said,
"You're both two of the best Marines I ever met.
But even a first sergeant can't protect you two

from the insanity you're about to commit. I'm just going to walk away and play dumb when they ask me later."

"Roger that, First Sergeant," Morgan said.

And with that, the first sergeant departed the area, walking away toward a cluster of Marines.

"Spread the hell out!" he yelled. "What are you? Crazy?"

Morgan and Dean watched him walk away.

CHAPTER 32

Once he was out of hearing range, Morgan studied a hill nearly two miles away, and the ridge that rose up behind it.

"I will not allow them to take her," Morgan said.

"I agree," Dean said. "She's good people."

"If we don't take this chance, they will never find her," Morgan said. "Or, if they do, it'll be too late."

"Yep," Dean said. "They'll either behead her. Or rape her repeatedly. Or both. And they'll put that shit all over the internet."

Neither man said anything.

"You think we should grab an MRAP anyway?" Dean asked. "I think it'll climb most of this ground. Get us to the bottom of the hill, or even the ridge?"

Morgan shook his head "no."

"We're going to be charged with enough already," he said, "assuming we survive. If we steal an MRAP and leave it at the base of the hill, it'll either get stolen or destroyed. And they'll add that to our rap sheet."

Dean nodded.

"Plus, if we take it, we weaken their defenses," Dean said, nodding toward the Marines still working on their perimeter.

"We have to do this on foot," Morgan said.

"How far to the mountain?" Dean asked.

"Probably a mile. Maybe a mile-and-a-half."

"Are we thinking clearly?" Dean asked. "We could jog that, but we'll be exhausted by the time we get there. In this heat?"

"We drop our flak and kevlar," Morgan said.

"Well, shit," Dean said. "Even if we drop our flak and kevlar, they're in trucks and we're on foot."

"They won't stay in those trucks," Morgan said. "They know we'll spot those trucks in no time at all. Either by drones or satellites. They're going to ditch the trucks. Probably in a compound."

Dean turned.

"Hey, corporal," he yelled to a Marine nearby. "Bring us a map."

The corporal brought one over. They both studied it.

There was indeed a walled compound at the base of the hill, before the ridgeline really started its treacherous incline.

"You think they'll have the Marines there?" Dean asked, pointing at the compound.

"Maybe," Morgan said. "Or maybe they ditch the trucks there and head up that hill? Or that mountain?"

The corporal looked at them.

"You two seriously thinking about going after them?" he asked. "There's no way you'd live. There's probably twenty or more Taliban."

"We've got nothing to live for," Dean said. "And we've been waiting for years for the chance to finally fight these bastards instead of just stepping on some IED that they've hidden for us."

"They will never expect us to come after them," Morgan said. "Not this fast. And not with a swift foot patrol."

Dean spit and unsnapped his helmet.

"The Taliban are a bunch of fucking pussies," he said. "All they know how to do is knock their women around and fight from a distance. You ought to know that they can't fight for shit when you get in their grill. We'll be all right."

"We're going to need this map," Morgan said. "You care to take care of our gear? Go store it in your MRAP, please. We'll be back for it."

"Or we won't," Dean said. "It seriously makes little difference to us."

"You guys are fucking crazy," the corporal said.

"We're infantry," Dean said.

CHAPTER 33

Morgan and Dean stripped off their flak and kevlar armor. They pulled boonie covers out and handed their gear to the corporal.

They now only wore their war belts, which had the bare necessities on them. The war belt was a padded, thick belt that had suspenders to help carry the weight across the shoulders. It included magazine pouches, med kit, grenade pouches, and a dump pouch (for empty magazines.)

For water, the two men would be wearing their CamelBaks, which had their own straps.

"Feels a hell of a lot better without all that weight," Dean said.

"There won't be anything feeling good after we've run about a mile or two," Morgan said.

"Let's fucking get some," Dean said.

"We've got a couple M4s, a few hundred rounds, and four grenades," Morgan said.

"That's enough to take on a fucking army," Dean said. "We're Marines. And we won't be spraying and praying."

"One shot, one kill," Morgan said.

They bumped fists.

Morgan turned to the corporal, "Two things," he said.

The corporal nodded.

"If we don't make it back," Morgan said, "then you tell Captain Tomlin that one minute we were here, the next we were gone. And that we'd just left our gear sitting where we were. And you, like a good corporal, grabbed it and threw it in your MRAP. Don't you dare say you know what we were doing, or he'll find a way to burn your ass for not reporting that we left the perimeter."

The corporal nodded.

"That's the worst-case scenario," Morgan said. "On the other hand, what we're hoping for is we find Lieutenant Flatt and the other Marines. That we rescue them somehow."

"We're not sure of that part yet," Dean said.

"This isn't the time for joking," Morgan said.

"The hell it isn't," Dean said. "If this isn't the time for joking, then there's never a time for joking. Hell, we'll probably be dead in a few hours."

"Anyway," Morgan said, his voice overpowering Dean's, "once we've rescued them, they will probably be in no shape to travel. They'll probably be pretty badly wounded. So, your job will be to stay on the lookout for any fires out there on that hill or mountain. Any big bands of smoke. If you see that, you tell the first sergeant to get a drone or aircraft near it. Immediately. That will be us, putting up a signal, and we'll be looking for an extract."

"Roger that," the corporal said. "Seems pretty simple."

"KISS simple," Dean said. "The way we like it."

Morgan jumped up and down a few times, checking how his gear fit; warming up his legs. Dean did the same.

Morgan checked his rifle, did a brass check (even though he'd done one before getting on the CH-53), and twisted left and right, loosening up his back.

"You ready?" he asked Dean.

"Hell yeah," Dean said.

"You guys are heroes," the corporal said.

"No, we're idiots," Morgan said. "But sometimes, there's not much difference between being an idiot and being a hero."

"And sometimes acting half-crazy and being an idiot actually works," Dean said. "That's what we're hoping for."

"Well, they certainly won't be expecting two Marines to come hunting them down," the corporal said. "That's crazier than hell."

"It is indeed," Morgan said. "Keep your eyes peeled for a fire. Even if we don't find them, we'll need an extract before it gets dark. And we're not running our asses back."

"Solid copy," the corporal said.

CHAPTER 34

"You ready?" Morgan asked.

"As ready as I'll ever be," Dean said.

Dean was smiling and Morgan was again struck by how loose the man always seemed to be. Morgan was the worrier. Dean, the easy-going surfer, figured it wasn't worth worrying about much of anything. Not even something as deadly serious as a kamikaze-like, suicide mission.

"We're going to get crucified," Morgan said.

"You think I care?" Dean asked, "assuming we actually survive? You're the one always worried about promotions and being so damned up-tight about everything."

"Well," Morgan said, "Sergeant Dakota Meyer disobeyed orders from a lieutenant to rescue his men, and the Marine Corps gave him a Medal of Honor. So, maybe it'll all work out in the end, if we get really lucky."

"With Tomlin as our commanding officer," Dean said, "I highly doubt it. But who gives a fuck. You've already gotten a Bronze Star, and we'd want someone to come after us, so let's do it. To hell with the consequences. Even if it kills us, I want those bastards to know that you better watch your ass if you fuck with Marines."

"Here, here," Morgan said. "I'll set the pace, since you're the better runner."

"And I'll leave the dead-lifting to you, if it comes up," Dean said, smiling.

"We'll stay a tad spread out, with you running to my flank, just a bit," Morgan said, "in case we run into any kind of rear guard."

"That way one bullet won't get us both," Dean said, laughing.

"My thought was more along the lines of wanting you to help me keep a good lookout up ahead," Morgan said. "I really don't want to run into an ambush blind."

"You think they're waiting on us?"

"Not a chance, honestly," Morgan said. "They'll never dream in a million years that a couple of crazy Marines will go after them. Especially on foot. The only response they're expecting is one that will happen several hours from now."

"Agreed," Dean said. "Let's get after it. Before they hurt Flatt."

Morgan set off, at a fairly easy pace. Probably about a ten-minute mile. Just a shuffle, really. But the heat was coming up, and this wasn't a race. They were running to their potential death if they didn't see danger first.

Morgan kept his eyes as far forward as he could. He was studying the horizon and possible danger spots. Places he would hide, if the situation were reversed.

His M4 was pointing down, mostly hanging by the sling; his hands barely on it. Morgan wanted to save his arms, for whatever fighting lay ahead, so he let the sling do the work.

Faint tire tracks scarred the dirt from where the trucks had retreated, following their attack. Morgan just followed them. It didn't take an expert tracker to see them.

The heat was getting worse. It was probably already eighty-five degrees. Maybe ninety. Morgan took a draw from his CamelBak. The water was still a bit cool, but it wouldn't be for long. He took another, enjoying the coolness of it.

He hated warm water, but he'd drink it when he had to. His breathing was becoming methodical now, and he could hear Dean's breath behind him. Focus, he thought.

He glanced back. Dean seemed to be handling the pace fine. And further behind him, he could see the convoy. Probably a half-mile back now. Someone had surely told the first sergeant by this point that two Marines had run off toward the enemy.

Wow. Was this fucking crazy? Or what?

Two Marines running away from the only support that they had, right in the middle of bad-guy land.

Morgan waved Dean up by his side. Once Dean pulled up next to him, Morgan said, "We should have grabbed a radio. Could have called in air support. Or an evac."

"Nah," Dean said. "I wouldn't have wanted to carry it. And I wouldn't have wanted you to carry one either. You're already slow enough."

"Asshole," Morgan said.

"You know it," Dean said.

"I'm sorry if this gets us killed," Morgan said.

"You didn't put a gun to my head," Dean said.

"I know, but it feels more real now," Morgan said. "Convoy couldn't rescue us if one of us got hit, even at this distance."

"We've been relying on only each other for awhile now," Dean said. "Nothing much has changed there."

They kept running, neither saying anything for a while. Just the sound of their boots crunching on the dirt. They probably should have spread out again, but there was comfort in staying together. It seemed more than worth the risk.

"Hey, asshole," Dean said. "Ever think that with everything we've ever done, every experience we've ever had, that all of it led to us doing this?"

"I have," Morgan said. "Maybe even us finding each other, when you were assigned to our platoon."

"Yeah, not many corporals are as crazy as me."

"Not many would have defied orders, either,"

Morgan said.

"Let's just hope this pays off," Dean said.

"We'll know soon," Morgan said. "I see the glint off some glass up ahead."

CHAPTER 35

Morgan and Dean jogged on, getting closer to the sight of trucks. They were perhaps a thousand meters away now.

"Let's slow up," Morgan said.

He pulled his M4 up and scanned the trucks through his 4x scope. The trucks were parked in a line, bumper-to-bumper along the wall of the compound that they had seen on the map. The trucks appeared empty, parked just a couple of feet from the wall. The wall itself stood probably fifteen feet high.

"That's a hell of a wall," Morgan said.

"I don't want to climb it," Dean said, looking through his scope as well.

"You see anything?" Morgan asked, giving the trucks one final go over with the scope.

"Nope," Dean said, lowering his weapon.

"Want to cover each other, and move in bounds the final distance?" Morgan asked.

"Nope," Dean said. "They don't know we're coming, and they're not yelling and hollering over there. Let's keep moving fast."

Morgan nodded, lowered his rifle, and took off at a jog again.

They shuffled nice and easy until they were a hundred meters away. From this distance, they could see the lines in the wall. They stopped again and scanned the trucks with their scopes.

"See the bullet holes?" Dean asked.

"I see 'em," Morgan said. "But I don't think there was ever any doubt that these were our trucks."

"Yep," Dean said. "Not a lot of white trucks in Helmand Province."

"And definitely not a lot in groups of four," Morgan said. "Cover me."

Dean took a good prone position behind his M4, and Morgan ran forward about thirty meters. Morgan took a prone position in a low ditch, fulling hiding his body. He covered the trucks and gate of the compound, which lay beyond the first truck, while Dean ran forward himself.

Dean stopped about twenty meters beyond Morgan and took up a position. Morgan took a shorter bound this time, given that they were nearing pistol range now. If it was going to happen, it would happen soon. Morgan didn't want long bounds. He wanted as little time in the open as possible.

They bound a couple more times until they were practically on top of the trucks. Then, they stacked and moved toward the trucks, weapons up and moving heel-to-toe, ready to fire at any moment.

Morgan was in the lead and he used his head and weapon to peer into the truck bed of the rear truck. It was empty, minus some old grain bags. He carefully checked the cab, and it was empty, too. Just a busted-up, dusty interior, with the seat ripped in several places.

The next three trucks were the same result. Each empty. Each one causing about five or six near-heart attacks for Morgan. While Morgan checked each truck, Dean covered the gate, which served as a major danger area. *The* major danger area since the flat ground to their left was empty. The gate was roughly ten feet farther to their front; a massive steel barrier on a hinge, with no holes or slits or ways to look through.

After Morgan cleared the final truck, he shifted his rifle's aim to cover the compound entry as well. It looked about one-inch thick.

To their left, there was no danger. It was open ground, just a few rocks dotted the ground here and there. But there wasn't anywhere for a man to hide. Off in the distance in that direction, the ground sloped toward the mountain as you looked farther in the distance.

"Think we need to get inside?" Dean whispered.

"I really hope not," Morgan said. "Two men can't clear a compound like that, unless we get lucky. Too many blindspots. Too many corners to clear."

"Plus we either bang through that steel gate somehow, and let them know we're coming, or try to jump the wall," Dean said.

"And when we land, they'll hear us and know we're coming," Morgan said, finishing Dean's sentence. "They probably have dogs in there. Hold on the gate for a moment."

With Dean covering the gate, Morgan stepped away to the driver's side of the first truck. He looked at the dirt around the trucks, trying to read the tracks in the dirt ground. He then looked at the tracks at the other trucks in the line of vehicles.

He couldn't make out much. There were so many steps and imprints that the Taliban fighters had disturbed the ground pretty badly, distorting individual tracks.

Morgan walked back toward the front of the gate. The ground was harder there, so he couldn't make out if the fighters had entered the compound or not.

Dean, his head still toward the gate, looking over the rifle at it, asked in a low voice, "Can you tell anything?"

"Not yet," Morgan whispered back. "Give me a minute."

Morgan retraced his tracks, but came up with the same conclusion. Then he had an idea. In tracking, once you've lost a trail, you make a wide circle and see if you can pick it back up. The wall of the compound meant that Morgan only had to make half a circle, so he made a quick trek around the trucks, searching for tracks.

And that's when he saw it. About thirty meters away from the trucks, the ground was a fine, loose sand. And in that small basin of dirt, he saw many steps. He followed it five meters and saw blood on a small rock. Fresh blood.

He touched it and his gloves smeared it.

Bingo, he thought. We've got these bastards. They hadn't entered the compound after all.

CHAPTER 36

Morgan jogged back, told Dean what he'd found, and the two quickly decided that what they were looking for wasn't in the compound: it was along the trail of tracks that Morgan had found.

"Even if most of the Taliban fighters are in that compound, we're here to rescue the Marines," Dean said. "Assuming they're still alive. And it sounds like they took the Marines toward that hill or ridge."

"Exactly," Morgan said. "Let's go."

They restarted their jog, following the path of footsteps.

"Looks like they're heading toward the hill," Dean said.

"Yep," Morgan said. "Let's run about a thousand meters and get away from that compound. Once we're sure we're out of sight, and any real danger from it, let's take a knee and do a quick map recon."

"Sounds good to me," Dean said.

The ground they were running on was flat and open. Nothing but dirt, more dirt, and a few fist-sized rocks strewn here and there. There was absolutely no cover or wadi's to hide in. But the ground up ahead grew rougher, and the land inclined toward the hill ahead. Already, the ground was increasing toward a five- or ten-percent incline.

Morgan didn't slow up until they were fifteen hundred meters from the compound. Better safe than sorry, Morgan figured.

"Let's hold up here," he said.

The two stopped and Morgan reached his hand out, "Let's see that map."

The two men took a knee, and Dean handed over the map. Morgan studied it a bit. They could clearly see the ridge up ahead. It was sharp along the top and wide; probably went for about a mile to their left and right. In front of it was a quite noticeable hill. It was about the only distinctive terrain feature in sight, except for the ridge.

"What hill is that?" Dean asked.

Morgan looked at the map, found it straddling two grid squares, and said, "Hill 406."

"You think they're up there?" Dean asked.

"Might be," Morgan said. "Or if they're not, we'll be able to see them from there. They might be in the little valley behind the hill. Or maybe they've already taken them up the side of the ridge."

"You think they're that far ahead?" Dean asked.

"I wouldn't think so, but they did start in trucks," Morgan said.

"Let's not waste any time," Dean said. "Let's get going."

"Same pace?" Morgan asked, taking a sip of his Camelbak.

"Of course," Dean said. "I could keep this pace in my sleep."

On top of Hill 406, Sayed Behzad stood with his men. He didn't know the hill as Hill 406. Hell, he had never even seen a map of the area. Couldn't even read for that matter. Like most Afghans, he was illiterate.

But, Behzad had grown up in the area, and to the locals, this hill was known as the "Hill of Bones."

Hundreds of times, the Afghan people of Helmand had climbed the hill and defended themselves from superior numbers of invaders. If any American troops were dumb enough to attack them today, Behzad and his men would hold them off no differently than his predecessors had.

Behzad had twenty-two fighters left with him on the hill. The return fire from the Marines had been deadly accurate; the Marine reputation for accuracy holding firm.

But the victory had been more than worth it. So many smoldering vehicles, their explosions caught on film. And the capture of three live Marines? Plus the video of the executions of so many wounded Marines?

It was greater than Behzad could have wished for in his wildest dreams.

Behzad glanced up at the sky. Though the top of this rise was called the Hill of Bones, he knew he didn't have to worry about an attack by the Americans. That was the least of his fears.

The Americans were always too slow to react. And they'd wait until they had overwhelming numbers and air support. Oh, they'd definitely come. They'd come in force to find these three Marines, but it would take time. Maybe a full day. And they'd be too late.

He looked up at the sky again. It wasn't the ground troops he feared. It was another drone. He could feel his left arm ache at the thought. Was there a drone up there right now? One he couldn't hear? He knew you couldn't always hear them.

He needed to hurry. But he also needed to get this right. The video needed to be perfect.

From the top of the Hill of Bones, you could just make out the smoldering hulks of the burning American vehicles. The vehicles had been built to survive buried IEDs, and they countered that threat well. But the Americans had never dreamed that the Taliban would have missiles to target them.

And with the fires burning in the distance, and with the height of the Hill of Bones providing just enough elevation to see the horizon, Behzad had the perfect backdrop for his video. He would now execute three Marines, one of the greatest terror videos since ISIS had burned a Jordanian pilot alive inside a cage.

Well, he'd execute two quickly. And he'd offer the third one to his men for some necessary entertainment. And then he'd execute her as well.

The Taliban had driven thick wooden posts into the ground. Beams almost four inches wide, eight feet long. Two of the Marines were now tied to the posts. Both of them were wounded. One with a badly wounded lower arm, while the other had a shredded lower leg. But tourniquets had certainly saved their lives. At least until they served their purpose in this video.

The first Marine was a black man. He was thick in the face and body. Well fed. And he stared at Sayed Behzad as the Taliban leader approached.

Behzad glanced back at a Taliban member holding a recorder.

"Is it running?" Behzad asked.

The man nodded.

It was time, Behzad thought.

CHAPTER 37

Morgan slipped back down the hill.

"We've found them," he said to Dean. "They've got the Marines up there."

"Flatt?" Dean asked.

"Yep," Morgan said.

Dean nodded, relief in his eyes.

Morgan had asked Dean to hold his position while he scouted the hill. Morgan had then eased his way up the hill quietly, peaked his head over it, and counted twenty-two Taliban fighters. Most importantly, he'd found the three Marines.

"There's a ton of them," Morgan said, relating the rest of his findings.

"You sure two of us can pull this off?" Dean asked. "Twenty-two of them?"

"Not really, but I'm also sure that I can't live with myself if I don't try," Morgan said.

"True," Dean said.

"In a perfect world," Morgan said, "we'd spread out. Take good, prone positions, and catch them in a crossfire."

"But what?" Dean asked.

"We don't have much time," Morgan said. "It looks like they're about to shoot two of the Marines. They're setting up the shot, video camera and all."

"Those fucking bastards," Dean said.

"Let's go do this," Morgan said.

Dean put his hand out in a fist bump, but Morgan grabbed the man's arm and pulled him forward into a bro hug.

"Keep your fucking head down," Morgan said as the two men held each other a moment.

"I hope you eat a bullet," Dean said. "I need the promotion."

The two men pulled apart and Dean smiled.

"If this is it," Morgan said, "I want you to know I love you."

"You're the only family I got," Dean said. "And if this is it, there's no better way to go."

Morgan grabbed Dean by the neck and shook him a couple of times. There was a lot more said in those few seconds than would ever be said in words. Both men knew they could die. Both men knew it was quite likely. And both men knew they'd take a bullet for the other one.

"Set out a couple of magazines before you start," Morgan said. "This is going to get nasty in a hurry."

Dean nodded, and with that, they set off up the remaining forty yards of the hill.

They jogged up the hill, trying to stay as quiet

as they could. And without all their armor, they moved like inaudible ninjas. They spread out a bit as they worked their way up, moving about ten meters apart. Dean pushed right, while Morgan stayed on the left.

The rocks on the hill were bigger. Basketball-sized in many places. Some as big as a man. Huge boulders, which you could hide behind. There were also craters, from past explosions from air strikes and artillery shells. There had been a lot of fighting on this hill in its past. That was for sure.

But one thing *not* on this hill were trees or shrubs or any kind of concealment (minus the few sparse boulders).

It was going to be a nasty firefight when it kicked off, Morgan knew. The Taliban would see them quickly. But there wasn't much time for thinking. They halted below the summit, crawling up the remaining distance.

Morgan was certainly thankful to have knee pads on. The rocks and hard dirt (from weeks of no rain) weren't exactly the most comfortable surface.

Morgan edged up above the rim of the hill, moving extremely slow. He first cleared the rim with his eyes, but then he pushed the front of his rifle above it, keeping it low.

The Taliban fighters had moved alongside both sides of the two Marines, standing behind them. The Marines were now tied to the posts, and they had the look of men who knew their fate.

STAN R. MITCHELL

How could they not? All American service members had seen Islamic execution videos.

It was truly every service member's worst fear.

To die was one thing. But to die on video? Where you'd be mocked and shared by thousands of fanatics? Certainly one of the worst ways to go.

The Taliban fighters lifted their rifles and started cheering and chanting. Between them, roughly in the middle of the hill, lay Lieutenant Flatt. She was tied up, as well, and half naked.

What the hell are they yelling, Morgan wondered? He slowly pulled two M4 magazines out and placed them where he could easily reach them.

He glanced over at Dean, and saw Dean looking at him. Two magazines were laying out in front of Dean, too. Dean nodded. The man was ready.

Morgan returned to the scope on his rifle. It was time. He pushed the selector switch off safe, keeping pressure on it with his thumb so it wouldn't make a clicking sound. Not that it would have mattered. The fools were still yelling and jabbering like a bunch of stupid assholes.

Too bad the next few seconds of the video would never go up. They were hamming it up for the cameras, like a bunch of under-aged frat boys who had scored two kegs of beer for the first time in their lives. It might be nice for the future jihaders of the world to see what happens when you leave your country and go fight against the West-

erners. Watching a bunch of impoverished, illiterate men, who should've been home providing for
their families, die at the hands of superbly-trained
riflemen might've deterred some future young
men from leaving their homelands.

Morgan had no plan. He wished he could have
told Dean to start on the right since he lay on the
right, while Morgan started on the left. But there
was no time for that kind of coordination.

The danger was too great. Any of the fighters
might see the two Marines at any second. They
were directly across the hill, still yelling gibberish
at the camera. Barely fifty meters separated them.

Morgan placed his scope on one particularly
mean-looking man. Guy had a thick beard and a
scar down half his face. He looked as if he had been
fighting for thirty years. He was the scariest man
of the bunch on the left, so Morgan decided to deal
with him first.

He put the top of the red triangle from his
rifle combat optic on the man's nose and squeezed
the trigger. The rifle kicked and the man's head
snapped back. Before any reaction could take
place among the others, or before they even realized what was happening, Morgan rotated over to
the left and started pulling the trigger.

He'd find a fighter's chest — no more head
shots now, not enough time for that — and pull.
BAM. BAM. BAM. By then, the Taliban were react-
ing. Trying to run. To locate the danger. While
they struggled with confusion and shock, Dean

was putting a hurting on them, too, firing his weapon on burst. Not typical Marine tactics, but it helped put men down for good and probably made the Taliban think even more men were firing at them.

Morgan saw a man go to the kneeling position, aiming an AK. He moved his M4 toward the man and fired twice into the man's chest. The man crumpled.

Most of the Taliban were scrambling off the back of the hill, but a couple went to the prone to take out the threat. They were firing. But Morgan and Dean were mentally prepared for this fight. The Taliban fighters reeled from shock.

Morgan lined one man up in the prone and fired right into his forehead. The other man fired off a burst at Morgan, forcing Morgan to duck back. He knew he shouldn't have pulled back, but telling your body to do one thing when it wants to do another isn't the easiest thing in the world.

But from behind the hill, he heard Dean yell, "Got him!"

Morgan pushed back up and ignored the fallen fighters, watching the only remaining men who weren't down running off the back of the hill for safety. Morgan somehow managed to get his sight on a man's shoulders before the guy disappeared. Morgan pulled the trigger, hitting the man, he thought. But the Taliban were gone now. All out of sight.

Morgan jumped to his feet.

"Let's go," he yelled to Dean.

They raced across the hill.

Dean beat Morgan across the distance and started firing down the hill from the standing position. Morgan reached the edge and saw the line of fighters running down the hill. They were a hundred meters away — Dean had dropped a couple who had been closer — and Morgan put his sights on the back of one wearing a pale-gray blanket around him.

Morgan aimed. Fired. The man fell. Morgan shifted to another man, who was wearing an old Army fatigue jacket. Morgan aimed. Put a bullet in his back, too. The man fell. Hundred meters. Easy shooting for a Marine. Dean had dropped three men in the time it had taken Morgan to drop two.

The Taliban went to ground and started firing back up the hill. Morgan and Dean pulled back, as bullets slammed all about them and zipped past their heads. They were well within the Taliban's range.

"Holy shit," Dean said, from the safety of the hill's rim. "What a turkey shoot."

"Every Marine we know would have given his right arm to have a shootout like this with these assholes," Morgan said. "Beats stepping on mines or walking down shit-filled ditches."

Morgan changed his magazine, and Dean decided to do the same.

"Think they'll flank us?" Dean asked.

"Normally, I'd say yes," Morgan said. "But I

don't think they realize there's only two of us."

"One of us needs to untie the Marines," Dean said, "but I want to get a couple more of these fuckers, so you go."

"I'll do it," Morgan said, pushing himself up. "We need the extra eyes and guns. But don't get too risky. We're lucky to still be alive. And I'll need you to help me get these Marines to safety."

"Hey, I'm not dying for no medal," Dean said, laughing. "I'll stay low. I promise."

And with that, Dean slid forward. He fired a few rounds and rolled ten feet over to fire again.

Plenty of bullets zipped past — and into — the ground where he had been. Dean had better be careful or they'd put a bullet in his face. But there was nothing Morgan could do. Dean took risks. The man lived for fighting and combat.

Morgan walked over to the tied-up Marines, keeping his eyes on the fallen Taliban around the beams in the ground; none of them moved.

Not fun taking a 5.56 at fifty meters, Morgan thought. He doubted Dean had missed many of his shots either.

Morgan placed his weapon on safe and removed a KA-BAR knife. He cut the two Marines down and said, "You men find weapons and cover these bodies on the ground. Also, keep your eyes on both sides of the hill, in case the Taliban comes back for more."

"Yes, sir," the white one said.

"I'm no officer," Morgan said. "Just a sergeant.

But you do what I said. And quickly."

While the Marines ran to find weapons, Morgan walked over to Lieutenant Flatt. She was laying on her side.

Her armor and gear had been removed, same as the two Marines. But her shirt had been torn off her. Her bra, too.

"Fuck," Morgan said.

He cut the tape that held her hands behind her back and said, "We'll find something to cover you."

"They didn't get my pants off," Flatt said. "But they were going to. The fucking bastards."

"They probably hadn't seen a woman in months," Morgan said.

"To be such religious people," Flatt said, "they sure act like total assholes."

She grabbed a jacket off the ground, shaking the dust off it and wrapping it around her upper body.

"You okay?" Morgan asked.

"I am now," she said.

Dean continued to fire behind them, but his shots were slowing.

"You're the lieutenant," Morgan said, "and thus in charge, but what do you say about us collecting up some of these assholes' clothes and burning them? Build up a good signal fire and get the hell out of here?"

"That's the best idea I've heard yet," she said. "But let me do that. You go check those two

Marines for their injuries. Patch them up as best you can. The Taliban didn't do shit for them and they're pretty hurt."

"Yes, ma'am," Morgan said.

CHAPTER 38

Two weeks after the battle on Hill 406, Sergeant Morgan and Corporal Dean faced a different kind of danger back at Camp Leatherneck. As planned, helicopters had rescued Morgan, Dean, Lieutenant Flatt, and the two Marines off the hill, shortly after the corporal from the convoy called in the fire he saw in the distance.

The danger from the fighting was long gone, but now their nemesis Captain Tomlin, aka Godfather, aka commander of Golf Company, was about to destroy Morgan and Dean.

Both men had been charged with disobeying direct orders, reckless endangerment, abandoning troops under their command, and even desertion, which was the legal term for unauthorized absence in a time of war.

They sat on two metal chairs outside Tomlin's office.

"If we're really facing forty years," Dean said, "then I'm going to jump across that desk and break his goddamn nose."

"We *are* facing forty years," Morgan said, "but he's bluffing. They'll have to court-martial us, it will take a lot of time, and we'll have attorneys. Right now, we just need to keep our mouths shut. Closed. You hear me?"

"I may still whip his ass," Dean said.

"You're not going to do shit," Morgan said. "I'm not going to let you."

"I've lost rank before," Dean said, "and it'd be worth it."

"I'm not allowing you to fuck up our case by looking like a deranged PFC," Morgan said. "Keep your head in the game and keep your fucking mouth shut."

"Loosen up," Dean said. "You're way too up-tight."

"I don't need to loosen up," Morgan said. "Instead, you need to take something serious for just once in your damn life."

Dean pulled his cover off, ran his hands through his long hair.

"You didn't even get a haircut like I asked you to," Morgan said.

"Chill, bro," Dean said.

"Damn, you drive me crazy," Morgan said.

"Nah," Dean said. "We balance each other out nicely. We're like the perfect match."

"We're not the perfect match," Morgan said. "We're more like a married couple who fights too much."

"Well, if that's the case, then you're the nagging wife who will never just let anything go," Dean said.

Morgan sighed, said nothing. You couldn't win an argument with Dean. He'd learned that already.

A few moments passed, and with it, the tension between them. Morgan was more worried about what might happen to them than he wanted to admit.

Dean asked, "You think we'll get out of this?"

"I think so," Morgan lied. "If you'll keep your mouth shut in a few minutes."

"I'll keep my damned mouth shut," Dean said. "Will you lay off the nagging about that."

They were silent for a moment, then Morgan said, "I'll get the damned media involved if I have to. And Lieutenant Flatt, and both of those Marines, have said they'd go to the press if the Corps tries to fuck us over with a bunch of charges."

Dean was quiet, spinning his cover in his hands.

After a few moments of silence, Dean said, "You know, the movies and books are all lies," he said. "In the movies, the commanders are brave. You serve your country. You win some medals."

"Yep," Morgan said.

"But in real life, you get charged for doing your damn job and the public almost never knows the real truth of anything that happens," Dean said.

"The only truth in war that I'm aware of is that the officers get promoted and those who are lucky enough to survive, are haunted for the rest of their lives," Morgan said.

Both men sat silently for a while.

"We were both damn lucky," Morgan said. "To have even survived. And with the risks we took? The Corps has to charge us. They can't have a bunch of men thinking they're Rambo and not following orders. Tomlin's an outlier. Most officers aren't as bad as him."

"Or as cowardly," Dean said.

Morgan laughed.

"I guess you're right," Dean said. "We took some risks. But it was the right thing to do, whether they burn us or not."

"It was the right thing if you knew the situation," Morgan said. "But only we knew, or could prove, that Tomlin would never scramble a rescue force."

"He did a hell of a job blaming us for being the reason he couldn't," Dean said.

"Of course he did," Morgan said. "He's a pro at covering his ass and fucking people over. That's how he's survived so long."

"Fuck him," Dean said. "I'd do it again."

"I would, too," Morgan said. "Even if it costs us our careers."

"Real war is about doing what's right for the men to your left and right," Dean said. "No matter the cost."

"Yep," Morgan said.

"Too bad in all of that shooting we never hit

Sayed Behzad," Dean said.

"I was too busy shooting at the mean ones," Morgan said. "And they hadn't told us at that point that Sayed Behzad was the man with only one good arm. Otherwise, I would have looked for him and dropped his ass for sure."

"I can't remember in all of the running around if I saw a man with one worthless arm or not," Dean said. "It all runs together."

"Well, it's war," Morgan said. "Nobody wins in war. We kill them. They kill us. And even if we had killed Behzad, someone else would have taken his place."

"Yep," Dean said. "I just hope we get cleared of these charges and can stay in. I love the Corps. I hate the Corps."

"That about sums it up," Morgan said. After another couple of moments, Morgan said, "The Corps. The war. It's changed us. Even if we got out again, you can't escape it. We're going to live with all of this the rest of our lives. Every night, we'll fight these same battles."

"Yep," Dean said. "We've tried being out. You can't ever get out. You can't ever truly return to civilian life. And folks back home, they'll never understand that."

"There's nothing for us back home," Morgan said. "There's just here. And here is wherever the Corps sends us."

"It's this brotherhood," Dean said, "that no civilian could ever understand."

"Yep," Morgan said.

"Well," Dean said, "no matter what, we hang together. We either get burned together or go down together."

"I'll drink to that," Morgan said.

"Hell yeah," Dean said.

He put his hand out and the two men gave each other another bro hug, holding each other in the hallway like long lost brothers.

Maybe this was what it was really about, Morgan thought. This brotherhood. This bond of being willing to eat a bullet for your best friend or those around you. That's what the civilian world would never understand.

"I love you, brother," Morgan said, caught up in his thoughts.

Dean answered, "Chill, bro. You need to lighten up. This shit is going to work out."

Morgan said nothing. He was worried about what might happen. And what would happen if he no longer had Dean to hang with.

Had there ever been a man he loved more? He didn't think so. No, he didn't think so at all.

EPILOGUE

The Marine Corps doesn't always get things right, but the story of Sergeant Morgan and Lieutenant Flatt rose beyond the reach of Captain Tomlin. Their courage and fast thinking were recognized for what it truly was, and Captain Tomlin's buffoonery and cowardice was heard in full as part of an investigation.

Morgan and Dean were cleared of all charges and Tomlin was removed from command. But the two men were not sent back to their unit, or to their remaining men. Instead, their story had gone high enough that they were plucked from the infantry and moved into the role of special operators.

They knew they'd have years of training to become certified, qualifying in everything from jump school to scuba diving, but for two trigger pullers like Morgan and Dean — for two brothers who sealed their bonds in blood and war — there was no place they'd rather be.

The End

Personal note from the author:

I hope you enjoyed "Hill 406." If you have, please consider posting a review online. There's no better way to recommend the book and help spread the word to others. (And a review doesn't have to be long or complex. Most of them are just a sentence or two, saying the book was good. Here's the link in case you can spare a quick moment to rate the book on Amazon: Hill 406.)

Sincerely,
Stan R. Mitchell

P.S. Want to talk to me directly? Email me at the following address: stan@stanrmitchell.com. I love hearing feedback, compliments, and even constructive criticism. :)

Other works by Stan R. Mitchell

Nick Woods series
- Sold Out (Book 1).
- Mexican Heat (Book 2).
- Afghan Storm (Book 3).
- Nigerian Terror (Book 4).

Detective Danny Acuff series
- Take Down (Book 1).
- Gravel Road (Book 2).

Other works
- Hill 406.
- Stolen Daughter.
- Little Man, and the Dixon County War.
- Soldier On.

ABOUT THE AUTHOR

Stan R. Mitchell considers himself an action fiction author, who writes exciting, fast-paced thrillers. Both military action and mystery whodunnits. He's also a prior Infantry Marine with a Combat Action Ribbon. Some of my favorite authors and influences are Tom Clancy, Vince Flynn, Robert B. Parker, and Stephen Hunter. If you enjoy them, then more than likely you'll enjoy his writing.

WRITING RECORD: Mitchell penned his first story at the age of nine. It described the courageous story of four young Native American men, who fought a valiant campaign against encroaching white settlers, after their village chief capitulated and signed a lop-sided, unfair peace treaty. The tale spanned more than twenty pages, and Mitchell has been writing thrillers ever since that day. Following a military stint (see below), Mitchell raced off to college to major in English literature. He felt certain this would propel his writing to higher levels and advance his writing career. Instead, he learned he despised most literature (excluding Steinbeck and Hemingway), and needed to adjust his academic plans. Mitchell would go on to excel in the University of Tennessee's journalism program, earning the Kelly Leiter Scholarship for academic excellence and professional promise in March 2001. After graduation, Mitchell published thousands of newspaper articles over the next decade, honing his writing skills during the day in the newsroom, while still hammering away on several novels during the late hours of night. He would exit the field of journalism to become an author in 2012, publishing his break-out novel "Sold Out," which tells the story of a retired Marine sniper, whose life is turned upside down. The explosive sales of "Sold Out" prompted Audible to sign a multi-book deal. Since that launch, Mitchell has drawn up more than a dozen stories. Several of these are in the publishing pipeline and will be released soon.

MILITARY HISTORY: Mitchell entered the Marine Corps in 1995. He insisted his contract guarantee him the MOS of infantry, and nearly joined the Army after the Marine recruiter claimed no infantry slots were available. After boot camp at Parris Island, Mitchell would serve all four years with Alpha Co., 1st Battalion, 8th Marines. Military peacetime highlights included: selection as Marine of the Quarter for the entire 2d Marine Division in the 4th Quarter of 1997; Honor Graduate of Corporal's Course in December 1998; promotion to Sergeant in less than four years in 1999 (no small accomplishment in the infantry). Additionally, Mitchell earned a Combat Action Ribbon in 1997 while serving in Albania, where his unit helped evacuate more than 900 civilians who were in harm's way (Operation Silver Wake.) Besides this mission into harm's way, his platoon also served as the Covering Force for a Force Recon team, which deployed with the 26th MEUSOC. In addition to working for a year with Force Recon, his platoon also had the privilege to operate with the Navy SEALs, training for Direct Action missions and practicing fast roping and ship takedowns.

Mitchell lives in Knoxville, Tennessee, and enjoys writing, lifting weights, and martial arts. You can learn more about the author at http://stanrmitchell.com.

BONUS
MATERIAL

Free preview of the mystery thriller, Take Down, which features a prior Force Recon Marine, who's now chasing down bad guys on the streets as a detective, instead of as an operator in Afghanistan.

PROLOGUE

I stared down at the text message in disbelief and horror: "Show up in ten minutes or she's dead."

And above the words was an image of my partner. Behind her, an evil asshole (who I knew all too well), held her in a chokehold with his left arm. Aimed at my partner's head was a big .45 Auto, held in his right hand. It was a Colt 1911 frame; the kind of pistol that's been killing folks since World War I.

The pistol held against my partner Colette had been customized and improved, but at point-blank range, it didn't matter.

I unfortunately also knew that the man holding Colette could kill her about a hundred different ways. With his bare hands. He didn't need a pistol with her unarmed. And frankly, he'd probably prefer to kill her slowly. Torturing her for days. The man was that depraved.

The brute's name was Sergeant Major Forrest Holding. He was a giant of a man, with an even bigger reputation for cruelty. Holding was a hulking, grizzled retired vet, and he was dangerous as hell.

He had seen far more combat than me, and he had already killed two police officers because of my investigation into Snyder Mining, a company he was affiliated with.

Now Holding had my partner, Colette.

The instructions in the text were clear: I had ten minutes to show up (ALONE) or Colette was dead.

I considered my options, but honestly, I didn't have any decent ones. The small town of Akin, Tennessee, where I served as a detective, has a piss-poor SWAT team. It would take them twenty minutes to assemble and gear up. And even once assembled, they weren't that well-trained. Certainly not good enough to go up against an expert Special Forces soldier with hundreds of combat operations under his belt.

I only had ten minutes to show up or he would kill her, adding a third cop to his long list of kills from around the world. And I knew Holding would kill Colette without a moment's hesitation. Worse, he wouldn't lose a single minute of sleep about it. But the truth was he wanted me; not her.

So, that meant I had no choice but to go alone – without backup – to face this dangerous monster. That, or I could simply kiss my partner goodbye.

Forrest Holding held all the cards, but I'm not a coward. And frankly, I really wanted to kill the bastard in the photo. I wanted retribution for the two police officers he had already killed. One of those police officers had been my best friend.

And deep in my heart, I knew I was the only man with even the most remote possibility of killing this man. I had served in Force Recon, the most elite Marine unit out there. And I had also earned a Bronze Star, which had been awarded for basically doing what I was about to do again: putting my life on the line in what was either an incredibly courageous (or foolish) act.

In the end, going after Holding might cost me my life, but this fight with Snyder Mining had already cost me too much. And the only reason Colette was even a hostage of this maniac was because of me. And because of my investigation, which she had warned me numerous times not to pursue.

So, yeah. You damn right I was going to show up alone. Fuck the consequences. Wasn't like I had a lot to live for anyway. I reached down and pulled out my Glock 19, performing a quick brass check.

If this man wanted a gunfight, he was about to get one. I glanced down at my watch, saw I had nine minutes, and sprinted toward my truck. Let's roll, I thought.

CHAPTER 1

There's no way I could have predicted the world of shit I was walking into when I sat down to interview as a detective in the small town of Akin, Tennessee.

Never would I have dreamed that such a move would nearly cost me my life. Multiple times. All within a few short months of taking the job.

But I'm not one to avoid deeply buried secrets. And once I began prying into the affairs of a mysterious mining company, cops would start to die and I'd soon find myself in as much danger as I'd seen in a brutal tour in Afghanistan as a Marine, serving in Force Recon.

It turns out that even in small towns there is danger and corruption, hidden under a thin veil of friendliness and charm.

And for me, what was supposed to be an easy year on the Akin police force (while I patched up my marriage) turned into quite a bit of something else.

But I'm getting ahead of myself, and no one

likes to have the ending of a story spoiled.

It's tough to know where best to start the story, but honestly, it started with the dullest and lamest job interview I've ever had. It's tough to believe how many big clues I missed in this tedious, monotonous interview. We'll see if you pick up on them. (I promise to tell it as accurately as I can recall it.)

"Danny Acuff?" the old Akin Police Chief asked, raising his eyebrows in question as he glanced up from a file in front of him.

"Yes, sir," I said. "That's me."

The old police chief, moving *very* slowly, nodded at my confirmation that I was indeed Danny Acuff. He paused, looking deep into my eyes, and smiling. It seemed a little odd, but I smiled back. His smile was as genuine, soft, and real as about any I'd seen in some time. I'd come from the hard streets of Memphis, so this was different.

Like any good detective, I studied him while he studied me. He was older. I pegged his age at around 65. Although he was soft around the face and even softer around the belly, he carried a thick head of hair. The hair was as white as bleached bones, found baking in the desert after decades beneath a blistering sun.

From the ailing and decrepit way that he moved, I figured the bleached bones image applied to more than simply his hair. He had the fatigued and tired look of a man who has had their chest cut open and their heart worked on multiple times. Even now, he appeared frail and underpowered: like a bass boat forced to rely upon its trolling motor to make it across a wide lake.

"You sure you wouldn't like a water or Coke out of our machine?" he asked.

I declined.

Chief Fred Bradbury struck me as more of a gentle grandfather or pleasant pastor than a small-town police chief, but I wanted the job. And I could deal with less-than-perfect leadership. I had experienced plenty of great leadership in the Marine Corps.

Police chiefs in Akin – a small town twenty minutes north of Knoxville – were probably less cold-shouldered than overworked police chiefs in major cities, such as Memphis; the city from which I was coming.

One other thing I noticed about Chief Bradbury was that he didn't move in a hurry.

He slowly returned his eyes to my file. His eyes tightened and strained a moment, then he reached for the glasses on top of his head. But they weren't there, so he straightened his full head of gray hair back into place and searched his desk. He moved some papers, struck out, then dug through another stack.

He found the glasses, looked back up at me, and smiled.

"I'm always losing them," he informed me.

I nodded, unsure if any remark was necessary

on my end.

To my left, a man shook his head in disbelief. The man looked embarrassed by the chief and had introduced himself earlier as the mayor of Akin. I thought it odd the mayor would be involved in the hiring of a mere detective, but this was my first interview at a small police department, so maybe it's typical. I didn't know.

"Goodness, you're big," the chief said, recapturing my attention. He was reading from my file again. "It says here you're six feet, three inches, and weigh 230?"

He looked up. He had seen me walk in and had even shaken my hand, but maybe he hadn't noticed.

"Yes, sir," I said, smiling. I gave him my best smile. "I require some serious eating."

"You ever play any football?" he asked, laying the file down, leaning back in his chair, and now positively beaming at me.

"A little," I said. "Played middle linebacker some."

He smiled over at the mayor with the revelation. The mayor looked like he was about to explode in anger at such a slow-paced, laid-back interview. The police chief missed the look, apparently, and asked, "How did someone your size not play in college?"

"I played a little," I said, significantly downplaying the truth.

"Goodness, you're big enough to play pro. You

get hurt?"

"No, sir. I was decent, but 9/11 happened." (Another understatement. I could have absolutely played professionally. Had agents and scouts beating down my door.)

"Is that why you joined the Marines?" the chief asked.

"Yes, sir," I said, thinking that at least the chief had read the file before I arrived.

He glanced back at the mayor, pointed at me, and said, "I told you this man was a good man. Would be a great addition to the department."

The mayor appeared unconvinced and crossed his arms. I hated to admit it, but I agreed with the mayor on this one. So far Chief Bradbury had determined my name, my height, and my football acumen. Oh, and my foolish notion of duty, and from that, he'd already decided I was a good man. Seemed a little premature to me.

Chief Bradbury had somehow maintained an impressive innocence to have spent a lifetime in law enforcement.

But he sat there smiling, clearly in no rush to continue the interview. "How come you decided to join?"

"I felt the old call of duty after the towers went down," I said. "And my Dad served in Vietnam, so it made sense."

He nodded. And would you believe he smiled harder? He was positively beaming.

He looked back down at the file again, his eyes

straining to read something. He looked back up. "See much action?"

For a vet, this question rankles about as bad as the offensive question of, "Have you ever killed anyone?"

I knew that since he had asked the question, he'd never served, and despite absolutely hating being asked these kinds of questions about my service, I was beginning to warm to him. His actions were so genuine and kind, that he clearly didn't mean anything bad by the question.

"I missed most of it," I lied.

He nodded a disappointed nod. There went his chance to hire a war hero and hear some good war stories on coffee breaks, I thought. Nonetheless, he knocked the disappointment away quickly and smiled again.

"I'm really glad to hear that. That war has messed up a lot of people."

The chief picked my file back up. Then he stopped, laid it down, and asked the mayor, "Would you like some coffee, mayor? Or do you need a bathroom break? You seem a little antsy."

"I'm fine," the mayor snapped. He glanced at his watch. "And I've got an appointment coming up, so if we could – "

"Yes, of course," Chief Bradbury said, returning to the file, but with barely more noticeable speed.

I liked the mayor's sense of urgency. It was more in line with mine. The mayor's name was Tom Follett. Like many mayors, he seemed to be in a hurry to make something happen.

Chief Bradbury was reading my file – SLOWLY – and though his leisurely pace was killing me, it was hard to get agitated at such a friendly soul.

The mayor probably tolerated him because the chief did not appear to be the confrontational type. Chief Bradbury wasn't the kind of man who'd stand up to a mayor and town council, demanding more money for the police department's budget that year. A useful man if you were a mayor trying to avoid bad press or tax increases.

If I had to guess, I'd say he was the kind of chief who was born and raised in Akin and had probably worked his way up from the bottom. Bradbury probably knew the town like the back of his hand and attended one of its historic Baptist churches.

"Says here after you got out of the Marines, you went back to college, followed by several years at the Memphis Police Department. Is that right?"

He was driving me crazy with the obvious questions. Of course, that information was right, or I wouldn't have put it in the file. But regardless of my feelings and my desire to speed this along, I swallowed down the agitation and smiled at him, nodding in confirmation.

"Any particular reason you picked Memphis?" he asked.

"They had a bunch of openings," I answered, "so I figured I had a good chance of landing a position."

The truth was more complicated. The fact was

I hadn't wanted to return to my hometown of Oliver Springs after college, which was a similar small town to Akin. A mere ten minutes away, in fact.

Damn, why was I back here? How had my life gotten this screwed up that I was now returning to the place I'd said I'd never revisit?

Don't think about it, Danny. Shake it off.

Unfortunately, Oliver Springs was a lot like Akin. One of those small towns where not much happens and everyone knows your business.

The few times that I had been given leave from the Marines, I had learned the hard way that it's true: you can't go home again. No one understands the military. The questions from well-meaning family members are too much. The church you were raised in is too small. The girls you once pined for have married or moved away or become far less magical than memory suggested.

I knew I couldn't move back to Oliver Springs after my time with the Marines and return to college ended. And I wanted a police department where I'd see plenty of action. You don't do two tours in Afghanistan, then quietly retire to some boring, small-town police department. Memphis guaranteed me some action and had kept me happy until my marriage apparently fell apart without me knowing.

And now here I was. Moving back to a small, miserable town, just ten minutes from Oliver Springs. All in the hopes of saving my marriage.

Damn, where had I gone wrong...

"You glad to be moving back home?" Bradbury asked.

Given how slow and unhurried this interview was going? Hell no.

But, the police chief was smiling again. He was like a gentle, slow-moving river. He was like the guy who sits on his porch all day on some country road, waving to passing cars headed down the highway. But I needed the job, and so I lied about moving back home, saying, "Yes, sir. Been dreaming about it for years."

That's how the interview went. Nothing but simple questions, which a ten-year-old could have easily answered. The whole time, Mayor Tom Follett stewed until he finally glanced at his watch a fourth time and abruptly left.

Chief Bradbury smiled after he had left and said, "Don't worry about him. He just doesn't like it when we bring outsiders in. Says they don't stick around long, and that they don't know our ways."

"I'm originally from Oliver Springs, Chief. I know the ways."

Lord, did I know the ways. This man would be inviting me to a church homecoming any time now.

"I know you do," Bradbury said. "Tell you what, let's dispense with the interview. I can see you're a fine man, and you're exactly what I've been looking for."

"Chief, I don't mean to be rude, but you've barely interviewed me."

The chief stood and removed his glasses.

"Danny, trust me. You're exactly what I've been looking for."

I left the office without giving that final sentence a second thought. I'd soon learn that though I'm a pretty solid detective, with a long and outstanding record, I missed some pretty obvious clues that day. It turns out that not everything in Akin was as slow and simple as it seemed. And my read on the chief, mayor, and town of Akin was about as off the mark and inaccurate as Goliath's belief that he could easily slay David.

And Chief Bradbury's statement that I was exactly what he'd been looking for? That wasn't just a clue. That should have been recognized as a giant billboard. A blaring klaxon horn.

Why would a small-town police chief hire a big-city detective? Who also has a long and distinguished war record? Duh, right? Because there was a massive case that needed to be busted wide open and a dang-near war that needed to be fought.

And yet I blew by that clue without noticing a single thing, thinking the entire time that Chief Bradbury was a simpleton and that I was about to get some easy income and time to work on my marriage. My, my. How wrong I would be.

CHAPTER 2

I drove home feeling thankful I had likely been hired, but a little worried nonetheless. I knew my wife Ali was going to blow a gasket when she found out about the job. Our marriage was already shaky, and this new job wasn't going to help things. But I needed it for my own sanity. That's what I needed to get across to her.

I pulled into the driveway of the half-million-dollar home that we couldn't afford, but which she insisted we buy. Ali was all about appearances. Whether it was our home, or our marriage, all she cared about was that it looked perfectly to outsiders. But the truth was not as it seemed. The financing of the home was on as shaky ground as our marriage. We had financed it when I was making good money as a detective with the Memphis PD. But now I would be making half that much, and Ali had been going on one of her quite-common spending sprees to furnish and improve the new home we had just moved into.

"These are one-time investments that any

couple make when they move into a new home," she had said.

"Sure," I had thought, but dared not say. I knew in two years she would be sick of the color scheme and need to have it changed or replaced.

I sighed as I parked my big, 4x4 truck in one of the bays of the three-car garage. I walked into the empty house and worried about the fight that would soon happen. I glanced at my watch. It was 6:19. She'd be home soon.

A bit of worry crept in. This was going to be interesting, to say the least.

I collapsed into our massive leather couch and flipped on ESPN. I tried to watch Sports-Center, and though the NFL playoffs were fast approaching, I couldn't pay attention to the TV. I kept checking my watch and wondering when Ali would arrive home.

By 7:35, I was growing pissed. She had said she wouldn't work later than six or seven. So much for that. I flipped the TV off and stood to make myself some dinner. As I walked to the kitchen, though, I heard the motor of the garage door groan.

I pivoted toward the door, opened it, and watched her park her expensive, brand-new 2015 BMW. The car was leased, and yet another thing we couldn't afford. She noticed me in the door and briefly smiled. She was on her cell phone, which she mostly lived on, when she wasn't at work.

She was always looking for that extra time she could be working, whether it was conversing with a client while she was driving or dragging her iPad into bed to answer emails. Everything was about billable hours for her.

Ali put the BMW in park, opened her door, and said into her phone, "Jenny, I'm sorry to be short with you, but I'm telling you we need to take this to trial. Give it some consideration. I'll call you tomorrow."

She hung up, pulled her tote bag out, and shut the door.

"Hey, hon," she said as she glanced down at her phone, checking for emails and missed texts that might have arrived in the ten minutes it had taken her to drive home.

"Damn it," she said, reading something. "I told them that wouldn't work," she muttered to herself before clicking on another email.

I watched her walk toward the door, and even in her hecticness, even with her barely acknowledging me, even with the fight I knew was about to happen, and even with our marriage growing colder, I couldn't help but remark at how beautiful she was. She was dressed in a killer business suit. Thin and drop-dead attractive, with long blonde hair that was the envy of every woman.

As she passed by, I kissed her on the cheek. And as she walked up the stairs to our kitchen, I noticed her strong, toned legs, and her best asset that rested above those legs, which the pants outlined nicely. Without question, her body had barely changed since the moment I'd met her, thanks to no kids, healthy eating, and a work pace that would put most ants to shame.

As Ali walked through the door into the kitchen, she placed her tote on the island and kicked off her shoes. She carried the Givenchy tote today. I hadn't even known what Givenchy was until a few years ago, but it turns out it's a designer brand that sells leather bags for $2,400.

Yes, $2,400. Believe me, you learn about a brand when it carries a price tag like that. Ali's face was still buried in her phone, reading another email.

"Honey," I said.

"Yeah, babe," she said.

"We need to talk."

"We're going to have to make it fast," she replied, laying the phone on the counter. She raced to the fridge, withdrew a store-bought salad boxed in plastic, and placed it on the island. She typically ingested her food within about ten minutes, all while standing at the island; Ali wasn't one to sit for dinner. Once she had eaten, she usually darted back to the office for a few more hours; or upstairs to her study to review files for half the night.

Yeah, this was the state of our marriage. Had been for years.

She had already ripped the plastic top off the salad, spread dressing, and placed a large bite in her mouth before she looked up.

"Honey," she said, exasperated, "spit it out.

I've got to get back to the office. We've got a court case that's gone off the rails, and I've got to review the changes on that Wheeler contract that came back today. They need them tomorrow, so I'm looking at a minimum of four more hours work tonight. What did you need to talk about?"

She stabbed another massive heap of salad with her fork and raised her eyebrows. Only when she ate alone did she ever appear so unprofessional and ill-mannered.

This was going to get ugly. But on the bright side, it wouldn't last more than ten minutes, because her work always took precedence over me.

Well, I had dallied long enough. It was time to spill the beans. I braced myself.

"Ali, I interviewed today with the Akin Police Department."

Alison stopped chewing. "You did what?" she asked, her voice cold and sharp.

"I interviewed with the Akin Police Department," I repeated.

"That's the most stupid thing you've ever done. If they offer you the job, you have to turn it down. I can't even believe you wasted your time interviewing for that. I thought that was idle chatter the other day."

I breathed deeply and tried to calm myself. This was how every argument went.

"Ali, even if I go back to law school, the semester doesn't start until August. That's nine months away. It would be stupid to not work until then."

STAN R. MITCHELL

"Your work is studying for the LSAT, dealing with the application process, and getting ready for the nightmare of the next three years of law school."

This was going precisely as I had expected. And feared.

"What's the salary?" she asked, relentless as always. "Thirty-five thousand a year?"

"Thirty-six," I responded lamely. "But we need the money."

"We wouldn't need the money if you'd already completed law school and were earning two hundred thousand a year."

I know she nearly added "like me," so I had to give her props for holding back despite her anger. This was restrained Ali, believe it or not.

"Not everything in the world is about money," I said.

She closed her half-eaten salad box and slung it in the trash. Typically, she always finished her salad. This was another ominous sign.

"You're not going to law school, are you?" she asked, her eyes boring into me. I was on the stand, and she was about to rip me apart.

"I said I would think about it, but you know it's never been my first option."

"Danny, you're smart enough and have the drive to easily finish it."

"It's not about whether I can or not, it's about whether I want to," I said.

"To not do so is underachieving," she said. "I'm

just disappointed you wouldn't strive to reach your full potential."

"I haven't said I'm not going," I replied, trying to calm myself. "I may end up miserable in this job. It's a small town. There will be almost no crime, and I'll probably be eager to go to law school by the time fall arrives. This is the final chance to get my love of police work out of my system before becoming a member of the bar."

Even as I said these words, I knew they weren't true. I had done one semester of law school and hated every minute of it. Every second, honestly. But I had stuck it out (because that's what Marines do) until my father received a late-discovered, fatal cancer diagnosis. I had dropped out of law school to take care of him.

Ali had continued on with law school, and I held off jumping back in. I knew I was in no way mentally prepared for the rigors of law school at that time, following my father's death. Instead of re-entering, I picked up a badge until I could get my head back on straight.

But a curious thing happened. I enjoyed police work more than I expected, same as I had loved serving in the Marine Corps. Thus, I stayed on as a patrol officer in the Memphis Police Department.

The income and insurance benefits were welcome while we dove further and further into debt for Ali's legal education. She believed – and so did I – that I would soon follow in her footsteps in the legal career. Her parents had certainly believed I would go back, as well.

Both assumed the two of us would one day take over managing the family firm in Knoxville. This would be after we had gained experience at a couple of prominent firms in Memphis.

But, my plans changed for good (at least in my mind) when I was promoted to detective after just three years on the Memphis PD. As a detective, I discovered my dream job, and I loved how each day was different. How each case assigned to me was a challenging riddle to be solved.

I threw myself into the work while Ali worked the maddening hours a new attorney works following graduation. In hindsight, I believe she didn't see how much I loved the job, due to her own workloads and pressure.

She had a bad read on the situation. In her eyes, she saw the hours I worked as pure requirements of the job. As mere duty of an overworked, stretched-thin civil servant. In truth, the job was a second love. And because it was a second love, I had no desire to return to law school. Why would I when I had already found what I believe I was put on this earth to do?

As such, excuses constantly popped up that allowed me to delay going back to law school. Once, it was a serial killer on a rampage in the business district of Memphis. He took me nine months of all-out effort to track down. Another time, it was a low LSAT score because I had lacked the time to study for the exam that would allow me to return to law school.

There was always something, and in no time at all, seven years passed. I had become one of the most-promising detectives in the Memphis Police Department, and Ali had become one of the best attorneys in her field.

That's when life decided to shake up our little world. Almost overnight, her father's health began to decline and we needed to move back to help care for him and take over the firm. Suddenly, everyone noticed I had somehow not made it back to law school. That's when the problems in our marriage had really begun. And her mother had done much to cause a good portion of the strife. It was her mother, even more than her father, who continually insisted I go back to law school.

"I'm so disappointed in you, Danny," Ali said, reaching for her tote. "I have to go."

The argument had gone as I had expected. It was just another blow to our already fragile marriage. She probably expected me to say something. To try to stop her. To tell her I wouldn't take the job. But she couldn't keep winning all the arguments, so I let her storm out.

If you enjoyed this preview, make sure you grab a copy of Take Down from Amazon. You won't regret it.